STILETTOS

STILETTOS IN THE NEWSROOM

Rashmi Kumar

Rupa & Co

Published 2010 by

Rupa • Co

7/16, Ansari Road, Daryaganj,
New Delhi 110 002

Sales Centres:

Allahabad Bengaluru Chandigarh Chennai
Hyderabad Jaipur Kathmandu
Kolkata Mumbai

The author asserts the moral right to be identified
as the author of this work.

Typeset by
Mindways Design
1410 Chiranjiv Tower
43 Nehru Place
New Delhi 110 019

Printed in India by
Rekha Printers Pvt Ltd.
A-102/1, Okhla Industrial Area, Phase-II,
New Delhi-110 020

To
My Parents

Contents

Acknowledgements

To say that I can 'write' — I don't know yet! But it does feel funny when someone calls me an author and if I am one yet — I don't know! Under this streak of under confidence, I do however know that this was a hidden dream I had lived with for many years . . . perhaps, since the time I first wrote a poem on a mango as a six-year-old. And, this dream has not been achieved in isolation. Many of my loved ones have lived it with me and still continue to do so.

Daddy, I would continue to be hopeless with roads, but with you around, finding out the right direction in life wouldn't be so difficult. Thanks for believing in my ability. Mommy, you've been my punching bag on many occasions. Wonder how you kept up with my madness? Thanks for keeping me so grounded.

This is also to the scores of friends and well-wishers without whom this dream would have remained a fleeting vision. Arvind Nayar, for being a friend and mentor. For pushing me to write when I didn't want to and for believing in me always. Advaita Kala, your support made all the difference.

And, most of all – Rajesh Menon, for being my strongest pillar. You were there when no one was. Sumit Yadav, who read my drafts and always gave an honest opinion. Chetan Pratap, for your guidance and willingly sharing a byline with me ten years ago. Hardev Singh, for being nasty and nice at the same time. GS Vivek, your undying faith in me surprises me. Deepak uncle, your scolding and love worked so well for me. Wonder how I would have lasted a day without JJ, Mishti, Goutam, Nilesh, Mohit and my little Anushree (Bulbul) – they were there when I did an unusual jig of laughing and crying at the same time.

Had it not been for my bosses and colleagues at different newspaper houses, my mind would have been devoid of any inspiration and enthusiasm. Thanks for making journalism a lovable (sometimes hate-able) profession for me.

This book would have been incomplete had it not been for those who came in my life and left even before I write this note.

Also thanks to my publisher, Kapish Mehra of Rupa & Co., my editor Rashmi Menon, and Kadambari Mishra for their support and encouragement.

Thank you Lord for making me your lucky child!

1

Day One's Dud

The buzzer announced the arrival of Kanta *bai* at the door. In between incessant ringing of the bell, there are occasional grunts of 'Baby . . . Baby . . .' Tucked inside her blanket, the 'baby' is in an ethereal world. Whether it was Kanta *bai's* perseverance or was it the electricity board's decision to provide uninterrupted power supply that morning which finally dragged the 'baby' back into the physical world, is difficult to comprehend.

I 'Baby' Radhika Kanetkar love to sleep, hate to get up.

'But Kanta *bai*, it's just 9 *na?*' 9.20 to be precise. The zombie, bedraggled look doesn't find any sympathies with Kanta *bai*.

'*Arre*, baby, it's your first day *na*. . . .' her voice trails of.

'Damn . . . Why couldn't that phone alarm work for once?' I stop. And then time it out. 'One hour to get ready. . . .

No . . . 50 minutes to get ready . . . 15 minutes to look for an auto . . . 30 minutes travel. Satya Sidharth Sarkar, here I come. Am gonna beat you to it by five minutes!' Timing out the entire schedule helped me be punctual. I had recently adopted this trick after reaching a few places on time. This was just a confidence-building exercise.

Satya Sidharth Sarkar, editor of *The New Press*, the oldest English daily in Pune, has a stocky built and a receding hairline, is pro-Bong and a thorough-bred communist. Fondly called 'Triple S', the last I heard was that he had sobered down and restrained on the use of expletives – fucks, *chuths*, shags and damns. Not that I care much, but I had heard it because there are more women in the Pune bureau and since when did women journalists abstain from using swear words?

But Triple S is cool and, to my chagrin, not on time. I really did beat him to it!

I chose a pristine white kurta for day one – a Monday – I auspiciously prefer to start any new work. I think I looked pretty. White always does it for me. A shade of light green on the *salwar* and *duppatta* were impeccable. Now it's like this – am not a journo who uses swear words as liberally, gives enough detailing to the way she dresses and talks. So, if not journalism, I would have opted for a career in personality development. Style guru Rad Kat wouldn't have sounded so bad after all. On second thoughts, Rat Kat wouldn't be a bad name too. For one, my hair is always playing the cat-and-mouse game with me. There are days when the curls set in naturally and then there are times when mousse, water, spit are elementary ingredients in setting my hair where it belongs — my head.

I am still waiting. . . . 'Now, what is this? He asked me to be here at 11 and it's 1.30! Is he coming, have you told him Radhika Kanetkar is here . . . is he. . . . ?'

I am cut short by the otherwise gentle receptionist. 'Madam, what's my fault? Sarkar sir often comes by 3 pm. You please sit here *na*.'

Ok, I sit. Now what? It's embarrassing you see. I hate to wait for people at receptions where every passersby's gaze falls on you. I am quickly losing it. First, because it's a newspaper office and my twenty-three-year-old mind is at its inferior best. 'Are they thinking I am an intern? Are they thinking I am the new receptionist or that I have nothing better to do in life than come and cool off my heels at some newspaper office?' And, second, my 2600 phone's battery is running out. 'How much more Snake II can I play?'

There are still fifteen minutes for the clock to strike three, when my only companion during the four-hour ordeal, smiles at me, and wiping his hand — he just finished his lunch, portions of which I was offered, and which I declined politely, even as another tide of hunger rose in my stomach — says: 'Sir has asked you to come in. Walk straight through the glass door and go to the second cabin from the left. OK?'

'*Haan*, Ok, thank you.' So far, he is the best thing to have happened on Day One.

Triple S looked like a man in his 40s. Spoke well and less. His uneven alignment of teeth has always distracted me. Didn't his mother pay enough attention when he was growing up?

'Sorry, got a little tied up.'

Four hours beyond the stipulated time, and a little tied up? I smiled. 'Yeah, yeah, it's perfectly Ok. I was here at eleven.' I grab the chair opposite his table and try to focus.

'Where is Chandrika?' Chief copy-editor Chandrika Reddy, forty-something, a pregnant blob of mass with a sullen look, rolled in.

Her eyes betrayed her feelings – 'Am not happy . . . I am frustrated . . . My job is thankless . . . My boss is a son-of-a-. . . .'

'Why don't you come with me?' That sugar-coated voice broke my solid chain of thoughts. Tch. I got up and instantly, I knew I am going to have a tough time in Chandrika amma's raj.

I followed her to the IT department, and formal introductions over, I was officially logged in as the employee of *The New Press*. I swelled with pride. Shit . . . was I in tears already?

Hey, hold on. If you thought I was lucky all the way, wait till you listen to my entire story. In fact, I hadn't been lucky at all. My indecision and lack of focus had put me off by three years. I was required to do a job of a twenty-year-old. After much rejection, dumping of CVs in the bin and a couple of internships and horrible psychotic bosses, this break with *The New Press* was **Godsent**. Never mind if I had never read the paper.

While many took 'writing' as a hobby, it was an achievement for me. Tears came to my eyes – was it because of the pride of having accomplished something in life or my sensitiveness, I don't know.

I trudged back to the desk and was allotted a seat in a corner. Jhumpa Haldar was welcoming. Sushil Sardanha was cold. Rameshwar Iyer was professor-like. I plunked in my seat and stared at a vintage computer with a black and white screen — perhaps it went with *The New Press'* office theme. I was nervous. I was supposed to work on QuarkXpress*, edit copies, rewrite them, giving suitable headlines, intros, design pages and make them too . . . Hello! What is all that? I had only done some freelance work on the latest summer footwear, Valentine's Day meal, celebrity interviews . . . but this. . . . And, I still got the job as a sub-editor.

Any way back? No. Alright Radhika Kanetkar, you better learn. Do or die! I mentally kicked myself.

Triple S had given me a week to learn Quark. Editing copies was not to be learned, it had to be adopted.

'*Arre*, but one week is too less *na?*' I blurted out to Jhumpa and she assured me it's going to be alright.

'I will teach you.' I thought I had found a friend.

Jhumpa was my age. And like me, she too was staying away from her family — she from Kolkata, I from Delhi. I started to look up to her. With her Bong twang and excellent English, she was in the good books of Triple S. She was quick with catchy headlines, popular in office and Amma's pet too. She was perhaps the only person on the desk who contributed

---

*QuarkXpress: Software used by newspapers for pagination.

to the city paper* and each time her byline appeared, I was the first to compliment. But this didn't last long. One week on, Jhumpa was cold. She had stopped talking to me and till date I haven't figured out why. Friends turned into foes . . . But was she even a friend?

Just three months in the profession and I had already framed my journalism rule number one: Never call anyone your friend, not so easily.

---

*City paper: Pull-out that comes out with the main issue but primarily caters to the city's news.

2

Me in the I of Me

I am Radhika Kanetkar, twenty-eight, work as a senior copy-editor. Right now I am sitting on a tight deadline and have three other stories, for editing, to follow. Am typing furtively on g-talk with one private banker, who I am currently dating online, and seriously hope to turn it into a meaningful relationship.

The scene played out in front of me is straight from a road side market. Some six to seven colleagues have gathered around a giant television screen right opposite my desk, discussing, debating, pontificating, and throwing up their own theories behind the double murder case that is hogging the primetime. Some accuse the father, some bring in a third person, while a few others have their own conspiracy theories. But I have nothing to say. Anyway, no one gives a damn about my opinion. My afternoon hours are hence devoted to my *Facebook* boyfriend Ashish Thadani, trashing useless press releases and thinking what I could do faster — typing messages to my darling or punching in the story, eager to be on the page.

It's been eight months in *Delhi Now* and I have already started looking out. I am told tabloid journalism is not my kind of journalism as am too serious for it. I wanted to yell back, 'Serious my foot! If you mix up profundity with seriousness that is your problem.' But, I still choose to work with a bunch that's indifferent and hostile towards me.

After facing extreme animosity from Jhumpa Haldar, it was now my turn to handle five people more or less like her.

The first three months were great. I was a part of the team. We spoke Punjabi English. I didn't mind when they joked about my car or my frizzy hair or the fact that I shopped in Greater Kailash. I never thought that was funny, but they did and so I laughed too. We bitched to no end about our boss with the funniest name — Shri Radha Shakti Barua. We called her Shri.

Shri was a fashion addict and as shallow as my group members. But basically Shri — four years elder to me — was good to me. She respected my work and liked me as a person. I liked her too.

My share of controversies had just begun. I was here for 'professional' growth, right? But that path to growth was beset with obstacles every now and then.

One of the top management bosses, Sudhakar Mehta, was particularly fascinated by me. He was twenty years elder and an admirer of Salman Rushdie. Sudhakar often spent ten minutes of his time everyday engaging in a friendly banter with me as he passed by my desk.

'So now you are his next, cute little target. Don't you ever entertain him,' warned Sonu Sareen, who was my age and extremely unpredictable. 'He looks right into your shirt so you gotta protect your boobs, OK!' came from Shri.

'*Arre*, but he has neither looked into my shirt nor has he made me his "target". Guys I can protect my . . .'

But the next thing I hear is that I am going around with Sudhakar. 'Naturally, some people are more blessed than the others,' remarked Salim Khan, which got into me like a prick. He and I handled the books page together and he was always wary that I often outdid him in stories and meeting deadlines.

Gosh! What have I got myself into? A web of controversies and that too with a boss who is twenty years older . . . what the hell was I doing there? I went into my shell and did what I knew best — work.

But that just didn't help. My much-younger, gay, pot-bellied, uncouth colleague, Rahul Verma, one day told Shri, 'Why is that bitch your favourite when she doesn't even do more than two pages a day? Leaves at eight every evening and sleeps with Sudhakar?'

I got these nuggets of information from Vincent Victor, a terribly unattractive man with a soft corner for me and the source of all the latest office goss. Sometimes, sarcastically, he would say to me, 'Well, you five-star woman . . . !'

But I wasn't a five-star woman! Radhika was sensitive, a thorough professional and reasonably smart. She didn't need to connive like Sonu, Salim or Rahul might have thought. Radhika was a fighter.

There were days when I regretted my decision to stay on in *Delhi Now*, and a tiny voice kept on nudging me to move on. Those days even my I-banker, gtalk boyfriend didn't hold any charm and I remained offline.

When I feel low, I always turn to my close buddies — Gyan Mukherji and Uri Singh.

Gyan was a year elder to me, married, and I can vouch that I haven't seen anyone as balanced and patient as him. And since he was a journalist, he knew exactly how the industry functioned.

My friend of eleven years was there on the phone and oh what a relief! 'Gyan . . .' And I couldn't control myself and burst into tears. 'Gyan . . . I cannot handle this anymore . . . they bloody character assassinate me, they hate me, talk behind my back and don't appreciate my work. I don't want to leave *Delhi Now* so early.'

The genteel Gyan gave me enough *gyaan* to take my confidence to another level. 'Sweetheart, gone are the days when you get stuck around with something you didn't like for long. Complete a year. Find something better. Move on.'

'Yeah . . . but . . .'

'There is no yeah, but Rads. . . . Hey Rads . . . just releasing a page, can you come online . . . ?'

'Alright . . . no problem!' But in reality I sulked. I really needed to know what I was doing and where I was going.

And just when I was lost between my sulk session and a page that I was editing alongside, the dear ol' Gyan pings.

Gyan: hey, Virgos tend to be too critical of others and themselves. Be discreet

Me: yes . . . need to tk charge of my life. i will. i am:)

Gyan: sure . . . remember you have just one life make it the best. No point wasting time over what others think of you

Me: ur rite. . . .

Gyan: Prioritise everything you WANT and go for it. It is not necessary you will succeed in everything . . . You can always say you tried.

Me: yes sweety . . . promise i will

Gyan: U are a sweetheart

Me: n u the greatest friend

Gyan: Really?

Me: mean it:) u know it right . . . i always turn to u when im totally depressed

Gyan: hahahah

Me: y laugh?

Gyan: found it funny, that's y

Me: reason?

Gyan: See you are a true Virgo . . . you want to know everything! Sometimes u want to laugh without a reason! Just like you can get worried without a reason

Me: really?

Gyan: Yes

Me: :)

Gyan was right. I did work myself up only to realise much later that the issue was actually quite trivial. I knew exactly how I wanted to tackle the 'devils' in office and even Shri.

Journalism rule number 2: Make sure you have someone you can call a friend.

3

Elizabeth is a Tarporiwala

Jhumpa Haldar threw that day's *Press Line* edition on my face. The desk was stunned. Reporters who sat behind our desk got up to see the punishment of the 'crime' Radhika Kanetkar might have committed.

My legs shivered like jelly pits. I had lost my speech and in spite of wearing this extremely pretty yellow *kurti*, I only looked at her with expressions I couldn't quite remember. All I remember was the heavy beating of my heart, a strong desire to become invisible and a wicked voice that said you were going to be insulted . . . big time!

I have this weird thing about looking good while being shouted at. And just in case you have people around to witness how you're being ripped apart, matters become worse. Let me explain how. They concentrate more on your clothes and you cut a sorrier figure. Confusing? Yes for me too. Anyhow,

Jhumpa was right there and didn't even care that Triple S was behind her.

'Read Page 3.' I opened the page, genuinely unaware as to what might have caused the outrage.

'Yes opened . . . now?' That was a cue for her to shoot back.

'Don't you even realise what you have done? Don't you even read the paper the next day? You have put some sidey old model Elizabeth Alex's picture as Lila Tarporiwala.'

'Oh shit! I didn't realise this!' But in reality I didn't even know the difference between Lila and Elizabeth. Amma had dictated some caption last night just five minutes prior to releasing the page and I confidently put this firang woman's picture in place of Pune's most well-known and influential industrialist.

'But I had asked Chandrika and . . .' Before I could go further, the witch charged at me with such severity that I felt I was going to faint. But I was still standing right there seeing them pounce on me one by one. I felt like a lamb without a saviour.

'And what Radhika? Don't you have common sense in the least? Don't you know who Lila Tarporiwala is?' I really didn't. I was only two-month-old in Pune and was unaware of anyone and anything out of the four mossy walls of *The New Press*.

And although I am originally from Pune, I was brought up in Delhi and moved back to my home town only for this job that I so badly needed. I was genuinely clueless about the lady's might because of whom I had not even sat in my chair so far.

Triple S had seen all that had happened. He called me in his room. I followed. The door was shut right behind. He asked me to sit on that rickety chair that cracked under my newly acquired calories. 'Tell me Radhika . . . what's the matter?'

I looked up at him with tear-filled eyes and said, 'Nothing sir. I really had shown the page to Rameshwar and Chandrika before releasing it. The fact is that I honestly didn't know who Lila Tarporiwala is.'

Satya's face was surprisingly warm — not angry. 'Are you aware she called me up early this morning and threatened to sue us?' The Page 3 stared right back at me. It looked like a masterpiece of a child who has just learnt how to write and paint.

'Sir, the paper will never be sued because of me. I will resign or personally apologise to her.' I had never seen my editor look so loving. Was it the yellow *kurti* or my moist eyes or my honesty?

'Be more careful Radhika,' was all that he had to say.

Once outside the den, for his cabin was so dimly lit — I wondered how he edited Page Ones and proofread some muck that reporters with a handicap in English wrote.

I entered the real den now. The Jungle wolves — Amma, Jhumpa, Sushil and of course, Rameshwar — were waiting to devour me. The former two chose to cold shoulder me. The surprise element was Rameshwar, who was waiting to reload his angst on me that Satya had poured on him early in the morning. 'How could you not know such a basic thing, boss?' he enquired. Now, what do I do? Gag this man's mouth, kick him in the shins or just play dumb. I chose the last option.

As he kept going on and on about the precision of my blooper on the hows and whys and whens, I stared at him blankly and wondered, 'Can someone ask this man to shut up . . . I had had this fill from Satya and Jhumpa . . . then why he is doing it all over again?'

Anyway, he did shut up and then it was the cool cat Sushil's turn.

Sushil's protruding eyes followed me from the time I walked out of Rameshwar's angry gaze to drop myself in my chair. And, as soon as I sat . . . 'Are you alright?' Frankly that was quite a relief since no one had really bothered to know how I felt. Perhaps my seniors just took the pleasure of yelling at me because I was inexperienced, seriously bad at editing and plain stupid with the PMC (Pune Municipal Corporation) or any city-specific stories.

'No . . . how could I be OK,' I stated with a smile.

'You wanna get some water?'

'Ah . . . no it's fine! Thank you.'

His eyes were still jutting out, but I felt strange carrying on the conversation further because I didn't need any attention from this man.

For the next two weeks I was not given any pages to sub, copies to edit and . . . people's hostility towards me continued.

Now, you ask me if I had a raging desire to rush back home to Delhi — yes I did — very very badly. But did I? No, I did not.

I came back to an empty house every night, filled with intimidating voices that echoed of Jhumpa, Amma and Rameshwar. I had started over-eating out of depression. Looked bloated. Unhappy. Inferior.

By now I had developed another defense mechanism — my journalism rule number 3: Aggression helps, suppression doesn't.

4

❧⁓ஓலஓ⁓❧

More Elizabeths were Lilas

Even after my first big blooper, neither did the self-assessment journey begin nor were there any signs of improvement. It's not like I had started editing copies with any special precision or that Jhumpa and Amma became sweet to me. I was soon to hit rock bottom.

So, eventually, from Page 3, I graduated to Page 2 of the *Press Line*. My editing skills were still questionable. I was given to edit City Briefs and they were the trickiest. Not only was our crime reporter, Aadesh Potliwala's English an apology, but he also twisted the facts so strangely that each sub-editor handling Aadesh's copies should be rewarded with a Param Vir Chakra. Had it been in my control, he would have been packed off to language classes, without his daily portion of bun *maska* he so lovingly bought every day from Naaz* bakery outside our office.

How could Aadesh write, I wonder? In between large bites from his greasy obsession, he punched the keys and filed the stories with butter-coated hands. Thank god, my desk was away from his and I never had to use his keyboard.

And, yes he was particularly pally with Jhumpa and there was not one moment when she yelled at him for filing copies beyond recognition.

'*Arre* Ads, come on dahling . . . when you are describing a woman you need not say — a woman. Rupa, who died on the spot — whose body was later recovered by the deceased's parents!'

That mobile lump of stupidity sucked up to my seemingly sex-starved colleague so much that he even got away with a mistake being pointed out in trademark Jhumpa-style — cut someone so sweetly that the person in question sees himself being chopped like soft chunks of strawberry. '*Arre chalta hai* Jhumps babe . . . such a small mhishtake *na* it is!!'

I desired to look at Jhumpa's expressions and what I saw was this: bun-*maska's* right hand touched Jhumps babe's hip and he rubbed it over and over and over again in such a casual manner that no one — not even the hawk-eyed Triple S would have noticed it.

Jhumpa had seemed to enjoy every bit of the 'lubricated' sensation . . . what with the fresh hickies planted on her neck

---

*Naaz: One of the oldest bakeries in Pune that was eventually pulled down.

and arms by her macho boyfriend, some Indo-American dude working at a call centre.

Not only did the lady enjoy utmost attention from Aadesh, the otherwise benign Rameshwar too seemed to fancy her. Playing footsie was their common past-time and despite their loud cheering and foot tapping, everyone around seemed oblivious – perhaps they had no option. Rameshwar was the assistant editor and Jhumpa of course, the hot chick.

But all this playfulness among colleagues was not doing me any good. On the contrary, it made me feel more wretched. I had made no friends in the last six months, my mistakes were ever-increasing and my confidence had taken a severe beating.

Once I left a headline incomplete. The other time I used a story as a brief with no intro, while the same story was being taken on the same page as a lead. On another occasion, I just went blank while giving a headline and the *baap* of all the humiliation was this – one day Amma asked me to edit Anu Awasthi's copy. Anu is a senior health reporter and quite efficient at her work. But basically she's headstrong and I have always felt that one screw in her brain needs replacement.

'Who the fuck has edited that Ruby Hall copy?' Naturally, Amma didn't even take a fraction of a second to point towards me. 'Walk up to Anu and ask her if something is wrong with the copy,' ordered Amma.

'Alright . . .' I answered meekly and frankly, I was quite scared.

But while taking this trip from one desk to another – which now seemed like a journey to Mount Everest – I could hear

Anu ask, 'Who the fuck is this Rads *yaar*?? How terribly can she screw up my copy?'

I tried to pacify her with the sweetest smile possible, but it wasn't going to work – not for this frustrated woman in her late 30s. 'Sorry Anu, it's my mistake. Just that I was editing a health-related copy for the first time so . . . '

Well . . . Anu didn't even look at me and headed straight towards Amma and commanded her, 'Listen Chandrika, you can't have these new, inexperienced jerks edit my copy OK . . . please take care of this in the future!' And the copy went straight to my competitor – Jhumpa.

That night after reaching home, I wanted to scream and howl – I felt belittled and insulted. I had no friends, I missed my mother's warm hug and I was a failure at work. 'How could I carry on like this?' I wondered. And made up my mind – I was quitting.

So the next day I decided to stay aloof, not to make any special efforts to socialise, do my work and head home straight. And I did just this.

Exactly a month from now, I almost got a job with *Poona Herald*. My resignation letter reached Triple S and I was sure I would be out.

He called me inside his cabin and I knew the formality of 'why are you leaving . . . where are you going . . .?' and all that will follow . . . but wait . . . Triple S just tore my letter and dropped the shredded pieces into the bin with 'Pune's Courage' painted in black on it. And as the last bit of my labour, taken to draft the letter, went flying down the glorified container, I looked up at Triple S with tears in my eyes.

'I don't want to work here sir . . .'

He looked up and gave me a comforting gaze . . . 'Sit down . . .'

I sat down and like a petulant kid enquired, 'Sir, why did you do that when you know how it is here . . . people are indifferent, I am a loser at my work and I see no future here.'

He listened patiently and then said, 'But your strength is your writing and you are excellent at that!'

Triple S knew about my writing skills because inspite of being on the desk, I contributed a lot to features and news reporting. 'But that isn't helping, sir. . . . I am mostly busy with pages, so cannot write as much as I would love to.'

Triple S took a minute's pause and said, 'Alright . . . just hang in there for two months . . . I will move you to the features desk.'

I didn't want to sound rude, but was scared to miss out on the job offer from *Herald*, so I nudged him further, 'But sir . . . what about the other job offer?'

'Radhika . . . say no!'

'Then no it is sir!'

I might have put off Prahlad Rawal, the Resident Editor of *Poona Herald* . . . but had no regret about doing that. I was with *The New Press* . . . the brand, the power!

From the time Triple S and I had had this conversation, I went on to serve the newspaper for four years. And, I would always be extremely proud to have worked with an organisation that helped me be . . . just when I was taking baby steps in journalism.

Mistakes are not glorified; rather, they are rectified at *Press*, and I had made many.

By the time I walked out of my adorable editor's cabin, my journalism rule number 4 was already formulated: sometimes one resignation letter can change your entire life . . . but mind you . . . only sometimes!

5

Such is Love

It took more than ten compliments, more than three rounds of coffee and just enough charm to attract Jaiwant Ranade's attention.

Jaiwant, who worked on the Main Desk, looked like a polo player that day and I told him so. 'Something new about you today, Jaiwant?' He didn't even hear that and naturally looked past me. Now that was by all means, embarrassing, especially because Jhumpa sat right there, looking at me from the corner of her eye and perhaps even wondering how I could have made such a 'bold' remark. Bold? Well . . . I have done bolder things, I thought, and didn't give up. This time I showed a little more excitement in greeting him. 'Hey . . . seeing you after a looong time . . . you weren't here?'

He looked up at me with a broad smile and said, 'Oh yeah . . . had been to Kolhapur for a few days.'

And that was a signal to take the conversation further. 'Really? Did you go somewhere else?'

'Oh yes . . . took a trip to the Konkan belt, covering Ratnagiri and boy . . . I haven't seen anything so beautiful!'

And just when Jaiwant was mouthing his travelogue so passionately, I realised how crazily attracted I was towards him. He went on and on with Ratnagiri, Konkan, food, booze, home, office . . . and I could only hear words! I was beginning to get extremely warm and suddenly aware that I might be staring at him in the eye a little too much.

Like me, Jaiwant was a typical Brahmin from the Konkan. However, there was a great difference in our upbringing. While I was brought up amid North Indians in Delhi, Jaiwant's academic and career life was limited to Pune.

In fact, he was not just different in looks, but way too different in everything — right from his mannerisms to his way of thinking. Jaiwant often looked like a hanger. He was so weightless that at times even half an inch of excess flab around the waist looked gigantic compared to Jaiwant's size-zero figure. I often teased him as *Undir*, Marathi for mouse. His features were disproportionately small for his six-feet height. Jaiwant's thinking was so different that in our first few dates, I felt outdated and like a living mass of ignorance and dumbness.

He spoke so passionately about politics, journalism, physics, biology, that little surprise, one day he pointed out, 'You are not passionate about anything in life . . . are you?'

That statement stung me. Of course I was passionate about many things, but didn't choose to speak as much as Jaiwant spoke about them. That statement was too offensive for me to handle and in the midst of our romantic dinner date, I accused him of being insensitive and 'silly' to point out such a thing to me. 'Jaiwant, I am suddenly so uncomfortable with you that it looks like two strangers have been thrown in together to share a meal.'

But instead of pacifying me, Jaiwant was reluctant to give in. '*Arre*, but I just said what I felt. You seem to have no ambition whatsoever. Basically you are a cute cold,' he laughed. Was this bastard here to make fun of me?

By the time we finished our meal, which I almost thrust down my throat, I was so livid that I staged a walk-out immediately. I didn't even wait for him to kick start his *khataara* bike. I was so angry that just after three months of being with Jaiwant, I made up my mind towards a break-up.

I am not the showstopper kind and had no intention to haul up the traffic, but when I turned back, he was chasing me. '*Arre* Radhika, sorry *na baba*. . . . Ai seriously sorry *na*. . . .' he kept repeating. People watched as I tried to board an auto rickshaw with a visibly drunken driver. At 10 pm, I couldn't expect anything better. Just as I set one foot in the rickshaw and the other one following suit, *Undir* pulled me towards him and I landed straight into his arms.

'Stop it you . . . what the hell are you trying to do? Why make a spectacle of this?' I shouted at him so loudly that some urchins actually stopped by to witness this scene that looked straight out of a corny, sleazy Bollywood film.

While the urchins giggled among themselves, I had no way out but to glide myself on *Undir*'s bike and zip off to wherever he was taking me.

We reached my house.

His coming up to my room was clearly not on the agenda. Yet, I didn't want to sound more rude by asking him to leave right there. *Undir* was behaving as if he owned my house. To me, it happens by chance . . . but I was clear the proceedings would not go beyond tea.

But then the shocker: when I came back with two cups of tea, I saw this six-feet tall, lanky, exceptionally bright journalist in tears! 'What happened, why . . . because we fought?' I asked with shock and disgust.

'Rads . . .' his face looked bloated with tears. 'Don't you ever leave me and go!' he pleaded. But this was clearly not in the plan again. Of course I was not in love with *Undir*, and was clearly amazed when he nonchalantly declared that he was.

I let *Undir* be that night. Primarily, because I was exhausted. Second, because I was really exhausted and my brain fails to function when exhausted.

My journalism rule number 5: Office romance can be fun . . . only if done with the right people!

6

Soul Connection

A month after my break-up with *Undir*, I realised I had a desire to let my hair down. I was in no mood to carry any emotional baggage, and for the first time I was determined to try out things I had never done before when I was with my parents in Delhi.

The first stop was Leather Lounge, at stone's throw distance from my office on MG Road. Though it was one of the most popular lounges in Pune, its entrance was deceptive. A winding staircase that made its way through several saree shops.

For my night out, I had invited Diti and Roli — jealous Bengali colleagues — from the Features Desk to be a part of the daring soiree but something in me told me they wouldn't turn up and they didn't! Was I happy? Yes, I found myself in my comfort zone. I was at ease knowing that I would not be partying with the people I am not fond of. But there was another nagging feeling in me — because I had no clue how silly or smart a girl looked while lapping up her Screwdriver all alone at the bar table.

I had already informed the manager and the tall bouncer at the gate to let me in. '*Press?*' he enquired in his steely voice and after stamping my hand with a beautiful horse (the lounge's emblem) I was free to enter.

From the galley-like entrance, where many couples stood necking each other, I made my way to the lounge. Usher's *Confessions* got into my ears and my eyes roved around the drunken twosomes on top of each other.

Psyche or scare . . . dunno . . . but all this while I had wrapped a black, shiny shawl around me. Perhaps, I wanted to give out a signal that said, I am not what you think I am. Basically, I wanted to convey that I might be alone but I am not here to be picked up. As the lounge's door shut behind me, my favourite Usher seemed closer and clearer, and I knew the shawl had to be done away with. I revealed myself: A delicate white, backless top, with a neat halter cut, tied together by an unevenly done shimmery thick belt. I stood pretty and tall in heels, in that over-used, yet fresh, fabulous top.

I was alone and delighted that I had become a part of the crowd. The track changed from my sweetheart Usher to Daddy Yankee's *Before the End of the Night/Want to Hold You so Tight.* . . .

I had no intention to flirt or even suggest that I am single and available. The whole idea was the thrill to do something I had never done before.

So far it had been great — the DJ was belting out a great combination of retro and latest Hindi numbers and the current one playing was the flavour of the season, Atif Aslam's *Juda Hoke Bhi*. Great music, great crowd and more importantly, I felt safe. No strangers had accosted me, no lewd remarks passed, I was myself, I was the crowd.

As I chilled out, letting the music and the Screwdriver work on me, I noticed a familiar face in the crowd. Our eyes met, but I was way behind in recognising that face, which was by all means very attractive. And, yes I noticed that the stranger was walking towards me. 'Was I going to be mistaken to be what I am not? And I was not going to take mistaken identity of a call girl lightly!' I almost muttered this to myself when he came and stretched open his arm.

'Hi . . . Rajat Mehta!' OK, so?

'Ah . . . hi, Radhika Kanetkar! Do we know each other?'

Rajat was accompanied by another male friend . . . Was he gay? I wondered. 'Well, at least he had a companion, I didn't even have that!'

'Ah OK, let me refresh your memory. We met at the gym the other day.'

'Holy cow, how could I forget, I had even enquired about him from a gym friend.'

'So you alone here?' I was somewhat embarrassed by that question. A, I didn't want to let Rajat know that I was so independent that I could gallivant pubs alone. B, I didn't want him to think that I was a psycho in my mid-20s, with no friends.

'Eh, actually I am new to the city and still exploring it bit by bit and . . .'

'Hey so join us lady! Come on in . . . meet him . . . Sameer . . . also from Delhi. So now, that makes three of us.' Sameer had a warm handsome-looking face and affable mannerisms. The three of us instantly hit it off well. To begin with, we had great common topics to talk about — Delhi, workout and music.

Rajat and Sameer as it turned out were great guys to be with. And since I am not the sit-alone-and-brood types, having the company of like-minded people was a great relief. We danced a lot and I guzzled down another glass of poison.

We bonded like brilliant buddies — the best thing to have happened since my stay in Pune and for once, I didn't feel out of place with them.

Stoned — the last thing I remember was being dropped downstairs by Sameer. I have no recollection of how I unlocked my door, for I insisted that neither of the guys come upstairs! You never know . . . jeez . . . the voice constantly reckoned me on.

The night was brilliant. I connected with the duo. I felt 'emancipated' that night.

Journalism rule number 6: Editing copies, giving headlines, smiling at seniors isn't everything . . . finding yourself . . . is!

7

Down But Not Out

I had spent nearly twelve months in the city and with *The New Press*, but my situation remained almost the same as it was when I had joined. Jhumpa continued to treat me like a piece of shit; I had made no friends at work and Rajat and Sameer's presence in my life was hardly changing the drudgery.

Amma's behaviour towards me was totally dependent upon how her previous night had fared with her husband and Rameshwar was as reclusive as ever. However, I had begun to sense that Rameshwar was — even if it means in lesser degrees — inclined towards me. Call it a woman's instinct or gut feeling.

He even helped me lay out a strategy to move out of the Desk and get an intra-transfer to the Features section. I thought my forte lay here and I was right.

The Features Desk or the 'Dream Team', as Rameshwar often addressed it, was full of girls. There was no single guy in the domain and, I guess, the girls loved it that way.

However, I was not required in Features when I was transferred there. The girls were curious about this sudden transfer. 'Has she been thrown out from the Desk?'

Sweety Iyer went around enquiring the whole day. Avantika Ahirbhoy, the Features editor, didn't seem very pleased either. 'There is not even enough room for all of us, so where does Radhika sit?' she grunted at Triple S.

Wow . . . now was I unwanted here too? I wondered. The feeling of being treated like an 'extra' is so unnerving that its effect on one's self esteem is excessively damaging. I was down but not out. I knew I could pull off my stint in Features very well. I had to; I had no other way, because if I quit this time, I better leave journalism for good.

Meanwhile, Rameshwar seemed more comforted than anyone else that I was in Features. Now, he had even started those initial *chai* outings with me.

I was doing far better here. Barring Sweety, the other girls were friendly; some were aloof and received equal indifference in return. Out of the many evenings, Rameshwar had asked me out for a *chai*, this evening too we made our way to Café Maha Naaz.

'So liking it here?' he asked.

'Oh I love it . . . I have already got three bylines in one week,' I said excitedly.

'Excellent!'

There was a silent pause in our conversation, like always, while speaking to him.

Rameshwar, 36, was a genius and I often wondered if he deserved better professionally. His *mooch* was an unmistakable part of his face and his big eyes were hidden behind his thick-rimmed glasses. By all standards, he looked like some nerdy scientist or a professor of Chemistry.

If things at work were showing up a bit, my love life was waiting to get that extra boost as well. While out of Sameer and Rajat, the former occupied a major part of my mind, Rajat and I were beginning to become great friends. He didn't understand a thing about journalism, but was a great critic of my stories and read them earnestly. Sameer, on the other hand, had told me once, 'I think, you have the prettiest set of eyes.' Our outings, which were often long drives to Khadakwasla and Lonavala, were perfectly timed — at the onset of rains, balmy weather or a 'fulfilling' day at work.

Sameer, however, was to be kept in the cold storage, at least for now. There were other urgent issues to be tackled — Rameshwar, work and putting my life together.

It was a particular evening, and one of the rarest ones, when we wound up early. It was 9.30 pm. Having loads of ads and classifieds is a blessing for us, especially on days we have fewer stories and more stress to handle.

Rameshwar bumped into me at the stairs as I hurriedly made my way towards Main Street. '*Chai?*' he asked. I didn't want to say no to a senior and definitely not to a man who had started showing genuine interest in me. But I did.

'Ummm . . . some other day. . . I need to buy some groceries, Kanta *bai* keeps chiding me every morning,' I blurted out.

'Oh! Come on will you . . . come, come be a good girl . . .' and he almost grabbed me by the arm and led me forward, looking around to make sure that no one had caught this touchy-feely conversation.

Café Maha Naaz was packed with varied groups, while the almost choking-to-death atmosphere was hardly of any concern to anyone. A certain Khan family sat facing the railing and slurped the *sambar* with two *vadas* dunked into it. While the iron trunk painted black read 'Khan' in Hindi, it did make quite a family scene with the *burkha*-clad mother of four who barely managed to eat, and the man of the house who gave out the orders. However, oblivious to this huge family, sat a cozy couple. They had chosen the seat carefully as it was next to the table-fan that gave out more whirring sound than air. While the girl, barely in her teens and wearing ill-fitting, silvery sandals, fed her beau chunks of *dosa*, the pimple-faced 'jaanu', as she addressed him, adjusted the Coke straw into her mouth.

Rameshwar and I seated ourselves opposite the 'jaanu' table. It looked like a safer bet than the Khans, whose children by now had started throwing around the spoons and *sambar* they wished to dispel.

We ordered our regular plate of bun *maska* and *chai*. Rameshwar is a sloppy eater. I was half-disgusted and half-scared of Kanta *bai*'s early morning ranting about not filling up the monthly ration on time. I really needed to get the house in order and stop seeing this man — my senior and my would-be something — eat.

The butter stuck on his *mooch* with disgusting alacrity and he seemed completely at ease with it, not bothered that he sat with someone from the opposite sex.

The long queue outside the café came to my rescue and the session that drifted from his family in Chennai to how Maha Naaz would soon be replaced by some fancy shop, came to an end.

We were home, my home, and unexpectedly Rameshwar asked for a glass of water. I felt slightly edgy. First, I had missed my grocery shopping and now, I would have to unwillingly extend the courtesy to him. I was in no mood for another round of *chai*, which he was clearly in a mood for.

I got him the glass of water (that he so needed), and even before he could place it on the dining table, he pushed me against the wall and gave me a tight smooch. I twisted, churned and even moaned. This I am sure, gave out a wrong signal so he didn't stop. While his mouth smelled of half-butter and half-*chai*, his tongue made it all the way down to my throat. I could have kicked his groin hard because that was the only organ of my body not in his control — but I didn't — instead, I let him sway gently on my crotch, kiss me deeper till his tongue almost reached my stomach.

He did stop after he opened his eyes. 'Hey sorry huh. . . .' My mouth was sloppy and wet, my hair dishevelled and my eyes blank. With blank expressions that gave a running shot from his eyes to the hard in between, I let him leave the door quietly. I even ran to the balcony and saw him walk till the gate of my Majestic Pride colony.

Sex or situations leading to sex with the boss is directly proportionate to where a story goes and on which page. So if the 'act' goes well, ensure a page one, if it doesn't . . . you still might get a page one. It depends on the act with *the boss* and *the act* with a boss.

Journalism rule number 7: Hold on!

8

❧

Some Respite

It was business as usual for Rameshwar the next day. He behaved as if nothing had happened the previous night and that we were the same old colleagues who went for impromptu *chai* sessions. I was disturbed at this lack of expression. I needed this man to emote, to either say sorry, thank you, love you, forget it, when next . . . something . . . but the moment he walked into the office, he was first hijacked by Sweety and then by Jhumpa and I obviously stood no chance next to them.

It was a day of remorse . . . I couldn't concentrate on any of the stories that I had pledged to finish. Sweety gave me a mouthful for having delayed a page the previous night and my ephemeral lover's indifference continued. Was I heart-broken? No, I was concerned. I was no longer sure what Rameshwar had thought about the previous night, if it would affect my job directly or would I turn out to be the long-suffering keep of an influential boss?

I was punching in a young author's story who had just come back from the US to help aspiring students get admission in American universities, when Rajat called and screeching into my ear said, 'Rads baby . . . we are off to Lonavala . . . pack your bags honey, coming to fetch you in an hour.' What?

'Nah . . . ummm . . . hey wait, what do I tell Avantika?'

'Tell her anything Rads . . . don't tell me you have never bunked office,' Rajat was persistent.

'No, hang on . . . you think it's so easy, huh? Cooking up a story and getting out and . . .'

'You are coming God dammit and all you have is an hour, alright! So stop arguing and start acting.' Click.

While the post-hang-up beep still echoed in my ear, my mind had already decided to play hooky and there was no better way than to feign a stomach ache. The sorry face did work, although the sudden raison d'etre was unknown and I was already putting behind thoughts of Rameshwar and work. As I went down the tobacco-laden, spit-stained stairway, all I could visualise was an auto rickshaw, a tiny bag to stuff my clothes in, green valley, cozy hut, hot *zhunka bhakhar*, Rajat and of course . . . Sameer.

I was surprised at my own speed. Not only did I reach home in flat fifteen minutes — a striking contrast to the thirty minutes I take otherwise, I had also packed my handbag with just the right clothes I needed during this short sojourn.

From the seventh floor of my building, I could see Rajat's Pajero parked outside the elevator. I also spotted a female figure, but was not sure who it could be. Not that the duo had introduced me to their bevy of girlfriends . . . yet I was momentarily curious. Momentarily because in the next five minutes, I was expected to get my butt out of the house or I would have to hear a voluble lecture from Rajat on time management.

A pair of jeans and three sweat-shirts is all that I needed and I flew down. In the spanking black Pajero sat the two and a pretty thing who was introduced to me as Tina — Rajat's childhood pal. There was no doubt Tina was beautiful, however, I was instantly wary of her. First, she wore a *mini* skirt for a two-hour drive; second, she carried a bottle of beer that was half empty and presumably finished by her because I knew Rajat and Sameer never drank while driving.

Smiles were exchanged and we were on our escape route from the world.

The journey was quite plain. Inebriated, Tina slept — with her skirt revealing her yellow panty. Sameer slept too. Rajat and I chatted, exchanging notes about career, love life and the world in general. I also whispered into his ears about Tina and if there was any likelihood of a romantic liaison, but all I got was, 'Nay . . . she's just a buddy! Don't be stupid . . . OK.' OK. I chose to bury the topic there, fearing it might upset my only friend in this date.

The rooms that were booked, were by all standards downmarket, although they were expensive by Lonavala standards. Tina and I were instantly put off. It was a large family room (I thought she and I will share a room) and the four of us were going to live together in the coming days.

While the sheets had cigarette burn holes, the toilet flush didn't work and the sofa creaked under the weight of anyone who sat on it. Yet, we were happy, despite the cribbing. We were together and it's all that really mattered. Although Tina's skirt was a nuisance, it invited greedy glances from the waiters, hotel receptionist and other pot-bellied customers who had come with their younger-looking girlfriends.

And, the skirt did change; only it was shorter this time. Tina had quickly changed into a pair of peek-a-boo shorts. Later, I even discovered that Tina spent her time drinking alone and to my surprise, no one, except me, seemed to object. 'Why can't you ever stop her from drinking so much Rajat?' Rajat, who was busy dipping a morsel of *zhunka bhakhar* in the molten white butter, gave me a stare, as if I had pulled the tail of a hungry dog about to put into his mouth a piece of chewy, chicken leg.

'Tina was in the rehab for almost two years. She came out four months back and has started drinking again, despite the many promises she made to her parents. Her father was so affected by Tina's drinking habit that he passed away last year,' Rajat was almost shivering. I thought he must really love her to let her be and even accept Tina — beautiful Tina — with all her vices.

I hugged my buddy hard and gave a loud moooooch kiss on his forehead. Sameer looked on and Rajat pulled him hard towards himself for a group hug. A tight one it was. I was instantly aware that this was the first time Sameer and I had come this close. The hair in my nostrils jumped with the sweet smell of his body and the strong spray that tingled on to my shirt for many days (or so I assumed). Our warm breaths mingled and we knew it was a bond that was going to last a long time.

Without speaking much, Tina had brought us so close that I had almost started liking this girl with a fetish for short things — short relationships, short naps, short hair, short sips and of course, short, really short skirts.

We rarely went out of our room and preferred to stay in the room playing either Monopoly or Scrabble or indulging in pillow fights till one of us pretended to be hurt and crying. If life in journalism hadn't matured my sensibilities before time and constantly nudge me to pretend, Rajat and Sameer and now even Tina, brought out the child in me — still unwilling to grow — wanting to smile for no reason, wanting to pull one another's hair, throw mock anger when what we cried for was not ours and still unwilling to get hurt

Life had given me much more with Rajat, Sameer and Tina in Lonavala, than what I had asked for. I had revisited my childhood and now I was steam-rolling myself to move ahead with the times! But then, I knew respite lay just a shout away.

Journalism rule number 8: Never mind if the stomach — aches are oft repeated, we all need a break and it needs intelligent minds to understand that.

9

❧

At Present: I was a Lover, I am a Recluse

Today, I am missing Sameer a lot. While the matrimonial ad had garnered tremendous response, I wasn't sure if I really wanted to end up with someone I barely knew. Worse still, I had to scribble out the details that I had always chided all my life. Journalist/fair/slim/good family . . . Hello! What was I getting myself into? I did the task mechanically, nonetheless.

Sameer's presence had given me all the comfort I needed. I had found love.

It was a Saturday and I had drunk myself silly with Sameer, Tina and Rajat. While we entertained ourselves with karaoke and jived to the classic old tracks, we were equally cool about the neighbours peeping out of their windows and somewhere, secretly wishing, that they too could enjoy life the way we did.

No, it wasn't that night.

The three stayed over at my place. We were so sloshed that in our drunken stupor, we unloaded ourselves at any available corner of the house that was visible to our hazy eyes. And, the next morning my house looked like this: Tina on the carpet, with a blanket on her. Sameer on a mattress, in the balcony. Rajat on the couch with his jacket wrapped around him and I on my bed, warm under a quilt — changed, rinsed and with a throbbing headache.

'How the hell did I even manage that?' I asked Sameer, almost panicking.

'Don't worry Rads . . . none of us got you into your night clothes,' he laughed.

'But how could I change when I couldn't even recall where my bed was?' I was almost in tears.

Rajat had woken up by now and butted in with a huge yawn, 'Sweetie pie, even before you got into bed, you remembered to rinse the glasses, remove your makeup, brush your hair and change into a night beauty . . . and yes . . . even cover all of us with adequate warmth, except Sameer, of course.' And let out an impish laughter, adding, 'Don't be embarrassed baby . . . it's just us! So be a chill now . . . OK.'

I sat on his lap and buried my face in his shoulder. It was so comforting that I didn't seem to mind the foul breath that his mouth so freely exhaled.

Tina had rolled out of her blanket and didn't seem to mind that she had (to my shock) taken off her skirt and what was more shocking was when the two men didn't seem to mind either. They behaved as if they had just seen a fly on their table and Tina as if she really was the fly. Tina looked beautiful . . . but, anyhow, the naturalist that she was . . . weren't friends supposed to accept us the way we are?

So after gulping down adequate lime water, Rajat initiated making a move. Tina jumped up, while propping up her skirt and Sameer chose to stay back. 'I guess I will stay on for some more time, the little girl has not been able to handle her drink too well last night,' he winked at Rajat.

'As if you did!' I blurted.

'Alright guys, you handle this among yourselves . . . we are off . . . bye love, take care.' I saw Rajat go down the elevator with the beauty tip toeing next to him.

I locked the door behind us and was extremely conscious of the fact that Sameer and I were alone together, for the first time. We were always accompanied by Rajat and somehow, I was comfortable with that.

But by now, I was feeling really unwell and asked Sameer if I could roll in? 'Of course you should, in fact that's what I was going to tell you.' With not so much as a thank you or sorry, I dashed off straight to my room and snuggled in the bed. I emphasise a lot on the Ps and Qs here because with Sameer I have always been extremely formal, extremely nervous and somewhat shy.

Once inside, my body felt heavy, but my mind was sharply aware of Sameer's presence outside. Just when I was turning from side to side, he knocked and came in (before I could even say 'yes'). The coffee and medicine were least expected acts of kindness from him. I simply thanked him and lay back again before asking him to bathe, if he wanted to, and take a nap as well.

It was well past 6 p.m. when I opened my eyes. The colony temple's bells were so loud that I thought I dreamt about them, but in reality, they yanked me up from my hang-over siesta. I quickly pulled away the curtains and saw the setting sun from my window. I was feeling better and the sun looked rather beautiful. I took a quick shower, changed into home-worn pyjamas, a timeworn top and with my hair still wet, stepped outside. I stopped in my tracks at the sight ahead. Sameer had prepared an elaborate Chinese meal, with cutlery well laid-out on the dining table. My jaw dropped open and remained at that.

'I could have offered you some wine, had it not been for your health, but how about some black coffee?' He looked so charming that I had the urge to hold him tight and kiss him hard.

'Ah sure . . .' I was in loss of words. 'But let me do it!' I said almost out of shame.

'I hope you like Chinese cuisine. I ordered the soup but made the other stuff on my own. The bloody sachets are so handy man!'

I couldn't speak, I kept looking at his face and realised that after all he was the guest and not I. So, I pertly got up to make us some coffee.

We chatted a lot over that. If we saw the kids jump into the society pool, we spoke about swimming; if we felt it got nippy, we spoke about Delhi winters; if we saw a group of attractive-looking girls pass by, we spoke about women in general. . . . And then there was this little silence. I wanted to hug Sameer for being there and taking such good care of me. But before I could do that, I let out a huge sneeze that almost roared in the colony. We both laughed and became children again. The tension had evaded within a minute and I was melting in Sameer's arms, almost suddenly.

No, it wasn't romantic or even mushy, we *walked* inside my bedroom. We hugged one another and when I did open my eyes, it felt like I had hugged him for over a decade. Then we kissed. He was tender and nibbled on my lips so softly that the sensation had already turned me on. Sameer took off my top and I covered my breasts, not out of fear but coyness. He removed my hands with his lips and kissed my breasts so hard that I almost let out a cry. He cupped them, then kissed them, then played with them till we both let out the giggle of school teenagers on heat.

'I must tell you that I love you and need you very much. Will you be mine, Rads?' I had tears in my eyes, huge tears that he wiped away, and kissed my forehead.

'I love you too.' He clawed on my neck and removed my pyjama and we were on the bed, making love.

Sameer looked larger when naked than when clothed. I had not felt like a queen in ages. Sameer covered my body with kisses, with a tenderness that surprised me. 'You seem to know just what I like Sameer. . .' He smiled. I moaned.

We made love twice that evening and ate food on the bed (much against my wishes) in the buff. Sameer fed me and I was not even allowed to take out my hands from under the quilt.

That night, Sameer went home to get his clothes and stayed with me for a week. Kanta *bai* was let off for ten days.

We explored every contour of each other's bodies, spoke about our lives, past loves and our future together. We were clearly in love.

'It isn't good, beta . . . write that you are convent educated, write how you look, write the languages you know, write. . . .' my mother's voice guided a harrowed daughter, who had the desire to *meet* a life partner, not *find* one. The seven-month long activity was becoming so cumbersome that I had almost given up the hope of marrying anyone. And, then I was a journalist who wrote about people and I was being subjected by the very journalist to do a job 'because she wasn't finding enough men, willing to marry her'.

Sameer left my mind not once and the 'editing' of finding a suitable alliance continued.

I was 29 now and some even claimed that I must marry before my menopause begins (anytime soon??) Yeah . . . right!

Journalism rule number 9: nah . . . no rules. Heart knows none!

10

Delhi Dares Me: At Present

I left Pune in November. I was doing well in the Features section and in the three years I had made meaningful contacts with celebrities, socialites, politicians, Ganapati Mahotsav organisers, sweet vendors, eunuchs, club owners, rickshaw *wallas* and even workers in the red-light area of Budhwar Peth . . . just about everyone was on my mobile phone.

Now, Avantika relied on my work blindly, although there were times when she would be at her worst behaviour, but on the whole, the tide had changed its course. I chose to change it. I loved Pune every bit. More so because Sameer and I had become inseparable, and experiencing the love he exuded towards me was more than what I could ask for.

But I had to leave the bliss. Not because I hated being happy but because I was not moving ahead. I left Delhi to rough it out in Pune and now I left Pune to rough it out in Delhi.

I was every bit nervous as I entered the Indira Gandhi Airport. 'Will I get along with my parents after four years of being away? Will I make friends all over again? Delhi sucks, then why am I here?' I had no answers to these questions that popped in my mind at every stage of the journey.

As I tugged along with two huge suitcases that packed almost everything that had become a part of my life in Pune, I saw images that were so vivid, almost as if the airport encompassed miniature blueprints of my beloved hometown. While on one side I polished off a huge chicken sandwich at Marz-o-rine, the other had a certain Radhika jump on *18 Till I Die* at a favourite Leather Lounge. Somewhere, there were also voices of chaste Marathi-speaking neighbours, Café Maha Naaz, M G Road, *kanda pohe*, rickshaw *wallas*, the dilapidated *Press* building, pot-holed roads, rainy drives to Khadakvasla, the muezzin's morning prayers from the nearby mosque, Kanta *bai*, Sameer, Rajat, Tina, Rameshwar . . . and in between all this . . . a lost Radhika.

'Radhoooo . . .' The shrill, loud voice of my mother was unmistakable. She spotted me among the hordes of other passengers that were trickling out of the exit of the busy airport.

I was home. I was in Delhi.

The glint in my mother's eyes was conspicuous. She had softened in the last three years, but the child-like enthusiasm in her demeanour was to die for. Momsie gave me a big hug, looked at me, smiled once again, got me into the car and out we were on Delhi roads.

I had not visited the city in four years, because I hated it. The restless, 'childless' and child-like parents often came visiting me in Pune, so I never had to bother filling up that 'missing' gap.

Delhi's topography had changed. There were unending flyovers and butter-smooth highways. The city looked a million times cleaner than Pune, — men seemed more robust than ever, and they looked like giants in comparison to Pune's not-so-heavy male counterparts. There were bigger cars here in comparison to Pune's roads, mostly laden with two-wheelers. There was no pollution, there was modernity, the women had sex appeal and most importantly. . . despite its many shiny offerings, my mind was happy — not for the city's lustre, but for Pune's murkiness because I loved it. I missed it.

The home-coming was that of an unprodigious prodigal daughter.

'Welcome . . . welcome . . . welcome . . . welcome Radhooo . . .' Popsie's voice could compete with his wife's. And, the already-hungry-father-filled-with-love had prepared a lavish meal for his daughter. There was so much to talk and tell, but the lunch went in silence, other than my brief description about the flight.

'I think you have lost a lot of weight Radhoo . . . now wait till Aishwarya stuffs you with *paneer ke paranthein* every morning,' Momsie laughed away.

My mind was already thinking about Aishwarya's *bai*-type counterpart Kanta. 'It's 3, Kanta *bai* must have finished cleaning the final house in the colony *na* . . .' I mumbled vaguely.

'Beta . . . eat first, the food's getting cold!' Popsie commanded. I shot a glance at him and letting another web of emotion make sticky glue in my mind, I hugged him. I had missed this attention for years and with slight guilt marking my tears, I told them how much I had missed them for the four years I was away.

Delhi now . . . home now . . . I didn't give my mind a single day's rest to mull over the already nostalgia-stricken heart.

First day at *The New Press*, Delhi tomorrow − I waited for the day to end, anxious about the new beginning like an 'outsider' here.

Journalism rule number 10: Who's to know if a decision is good or bad? Make one anyway!

11

Salman's Girlfriends and Udupi

The New Press building in Pune is nothing compared to the one in Delhi. To begin with, the former had paint peeling off its walls; the toilets were shabby. We feared bursting our bladders. The atmosphere was staid, with cubicles lined one next to the other. One look at this plush office that stands tall at the busy service lane of ITO and I thought the effort of moving to Delhi was worth it!

I was greeted by Ishita Kapoor — the features editor. And, like the buildings — Ishita Kapoor and Avantika Ahirbhoy were no match. While the latter was a vintage version of a scribe, the former looked like she's straight out of a prêt-a-porter summer collection. Ishita had oodles of sex appeal and an accent to make her look every bit unfit for this profession.

'Hi . . . you are Radhika, right?' She demanded in the most American-bred manner.

'Hi . . . yeah, I am Radhika,' I grinned under the uneasiness of a not-so-accented-a-language.

'OK, listen . . . come for the meeting right away and then we split, fine? Full page ads today . . . so you are lucky, no work.'

I smiled and followed her to T. Rajaraman and Akhilesh Chaubey's cabin. I was not as nervous to meet my senior bosses as much as not knowing what 'split' meant, especially in this context.

Just as my mind was rummaging through the possible synonyms for this word, I was led into a place that looked nothing short of a five-star hotel suite. Akhilesh, the deputy editor was clearly the king. On the walls were pictures of his teenage son and paintings, his desk was flooded with vases sans flowers, fruit baskets and imported cigarette packets. We girls, ten in number, occupied the couch, right in front of him and it sunk almost to the floor, reeling under our weight. I feared my zipper would burst open, as my tummy spilled out of my jeans. 'Momsie says I look thin, but the embarrassing garment has another story to tell . . . what the fuck . . .' my inner monologue blurted out.

'What the fuck? What's going on in this God-damned office man?' Was there a clairvoyant in this room, who could read the language of my mind? How did someone know how I was feeling? I looked up and saw a messy figure of a woman, for whom 'fuck' was the anthem. Kirti Karunesh (fuck) Chautala, the weekend pages editor was an ugly, disapproving version of Ishita. Her mass of hair covered her obscenely tight shirt that let out her hanging boobs so strategically that one wondered how she managed to reveal her cleavage so cleverly.

'It doesn't work this way Raja . . .' Was she talking to her puppy? No, it was T. Rajaraman, the managing editor. 'The full page ads have been taken off our pages and given to the Features people. Now, how am I to fill the pages at such a short notice? This is no fucking way to do things . . .' she only stopped when 'Raja' promised to generate stories for the six pages to be filled.

And then 'Raja' who looked like a benevolent, dark giant continued, 'This is Radhika Kanetkar. She worked with us in Pune and will now be a part of the Delhi bureau.' Everyone in the room looked at me. I presented my best smile, while some returned my smile, others turned away without so much as an acknowledgement.

Obviously, Kirti (I knew I had to call her 'misscrew' pronounced: miss screw) didn't care who I was or whether I came from Pune or Peshawar. 'Come on Raja, I don't care who this girl is . . . I just care about how on earth my pages are gonna be filled.' To Akhilesh too, it didn't matter whether Kirti threw a fit or took off her shirt and performed a nude dance. He was as disinterested as Raja and so were the others in the room.

One hour into the 'dummy session' and nothing concrete had come out of it. We were where we had started – futile chit-chat, latest yachts, Bollywood affairs, Delhiites' latest quirks and how we could improve the pages. I expected someone to at least ask for my suggestions, but no one did. No one bothered. I instantly felt a pang of indifference, not to say that the Pune bureau was any bit friendlier.

Out of Akhilesh's designer suite, I breathed a sigh of relief, thanking God for the adjourned meeting. And, then there was another explosion by Ishita. 'I don't understand why Katrina would hook up with Salman?' This she muttered while frantically touching the screen of her I-phone. We all waited in silence for her to mouth more such lines. 'She's a kid and Salman's attitude sucks. It's not funny how he flirted with me during his beach party in Goa. He wouldn't keep his eyes off me. I obviously refrained from talking to him. Who wants to speak to a man who's dated soooo many women? He even invited me home. I declined. He keeps messaging me almost every alternate day. . .' Ishita could have gone on and on, while her eyes were still on her latest acquisition.

'Yeah man . . . that fucking bastard, he's a bloody *chuth yaar . . . bhain chuth . . . arre* he almost grabbed me during my last interview with him. Had it not been for the photographers, I would have been trapped by his *tharki* advances.' Misscrew had already lit her second cigarette even before she finished her sentences, pregnant with long pauses, puffs and high drama.

The two bereaved girlfriends did stop, but only after it left me with doubts about their 'split' personality status. Is that what makes the word 'spilt' so dear to Ishita?

To my bemusement, no girl. . . in fact nobody reacted to this schizophrenic exchange of dialogues. 'Were they so used to it every day that they feigned ignorance or that's how big bosses in Delhi are supposed to be?' While losing myself to these thoughts, Sushmita Dewan, my colleague and the more affable among the lot, asked me if I would like some coffee. 'Ah . . . yes yes . . . and may be some grub too.' I so badly needed to feel normal again.

After a quick smoke, we headed to the closest and the only restaurant at ITO – Udupi. Once there, I thought Sushmita might have a lot to bitch about. Surprisingly, this very-attractive, very-Delhi Bong, guarded herself from sharing any personal information too soon. We spoke about the city in general and about how Udupi is the only place where we can get food any time of the day. Despite its dim surroundings, I already liked that place very much. At least it made me feel the average me again. I didn't want to belong to the league of Salman and Katrina. I didn't care who did what.

Journalism rule number 11: Take good food breaks to calm your senses.

12

❦

Writing . . . Who You? Part-I

It was the kind of assignment you would like to go for only if the ex-pat community intrigued you. I was the latest entrant so obviously, it was not difficult for Ishita to choose me over the others. And, when there are no interns and you are doing the Alice-in-Wonderland jig, you most certainly are the immediate target.

'Hey Radhika . . . you like mingling with the foreigners?' enquired Ishita.

Did I have a choice to say no? 'Yeah . . . noo . . . like it's kinda OK. . . .'

'OK, whatever. You go for this thing in the evening. The Israeli community in Delhi is celebrating something, so go for it,' she ordered.

'What? How am I supposed to make anything out of it? Celebrating what? Where? When? Why? How?' I wondered.

Did the five Ws and one H in journalism apply to Ishita?

'OK . . . here's the name of the guy and the complete address. Somewhere in Paharganj OK. Take John for the photo shoot. And, listen, once you are done . . . just split. No need to come back.'

Yeah, thanks. At least she gave me the address and I had to head for some place in Paharganj, for some celebration and was supposed to meet some Israeli. Wow. And, mind you, I had to drive there on my own. The directionally-challenged me was already shuddering and driving at night made matters worse.

'Alright I will manage this!' I assured Ishita, who was already looking at me suspiciously, for my lack of confidence and inclination in handling this assignment. This brief given, Ishita was on her way with her to-die-for Manish Arora's fish fry. I really did like her for the sheer exuberance she radiated and hated her for the sheer vagueness she *always* radiated.

What I liked about myself best was the ability to get right things done, at the right time. I pleased John with a packet of cigarettes, coffee, a promise for lunch, and my driving was taken care of. He willingly volunteered to drive me down to Paharganj and back to the office.

As we maneuvered our way through the serpentine bylanes of Paharganj, someone from behind tapped Mickey Staaik's shoulder vigorously. 'Shalom! Sir Hashish, sir, anything I could do for you?' The 'some' Israeli I was instructed to meet, turned a deaf ear, shrugged and made a quick dash towards a *gali* that looked so typical with dangling electric wires and hundreds of vendors who surround you and speak better Hebrew than English.

Mickey led us to Hare Rama Guest House where hordes of exotic-looking young Israelis were celebrating Hanukkah. He explained what the festival is all about. I nodded as I enjoyed the loud sounds of duff and drums and John frantically clicked pictures of women dancing and posing their henna-adorned palms and shining *bindis*. However, John was especially smitten by the matted hair-do of the men and he clicked them in various poses — something I thought was not required — but I refrained from giving instructions as I needed him to drive me back.

Other than the usual song and dance, there was nothing much I could carry back to write about. Mickey was not very friendly either. So, I left after exchanging numbers with him while he kept asking me how the story would be written. 'I think I know my job better. And, by the way, I will write what I feel like, not what you want to read,' I finally retorted sternly before I exited. As John reversed the car, I could see a changed Mickey, with his smile covering his hurt expression.

Ishita still had no clue about how the story had to be written and I was left wondering about its peg. I was confident, she would love my work, but I had a lot of unlearning and relearning to do. She made me sit next to her and changed every line, hacked every paragraph.

'You do know how to write, do you?'

I smiled.

'Not a single line is making sense.'

It would have, if only I had been told what I was supposed to peg my story on.

'Listen . . . you have got to rewrite your copy!' She spoke as she multitasked — sending text messages from her latest gadget, editing my copy and adjusting her rock-sized diamond ring.

I was quiet. I was told I write well, but Ishita had another version to give.

Sushmita was around and looked at me from the corner of her eye.

By now Ishita was bobbing her head so furtively that I feared she might rap my knuckles like a schoolteacher. She had changed the entire copy and it obviously didn't seem like I had written it. The 400-word copy was mercilessly brought down to 150. So a brief with a byline! That was even more humiliating.

After the animated dressing down, she left with misscrew for a smoke.

I turned to Sushmita, who dragged me out of the room.

'See, baby, you will have to be a toughie to face this. Don't forget, you are yet to prove to her that you do know your job well,' Sushmita advised.

I was still quiet.

'I know how it feels . . . but trust me baby; all of us have been through this. You know, you might be the best, but you have to go all out to tell the world, that you are . . . !'

I looked at Sushmita, whose concern seemed so genuine. It

felt like I had known this girl for ages and she was here to protect me.

'I will be alright Sush . . .' I felt really better to know that someone cared.

'You have got to be baby . . . or sit at home . . . playing with your mom's apron.'

I laughed and she lit her third cigarette.

Back to the news room, Ishita and misscrew romped around flirting with Bhaumik Mathur, the edit page in-charge, who I felt looked stunning.

Ishita came back singing and even cracked a joke with me, as if nothing had happened an hour back. I was still to get used to these shifting emotions. What's worse — I laughed at her joke and was already preparing for my next assignment.

Journalism rule number 12: You might be the best, but you have to go all out to tell the world, that you are (says Sush).

13

Writing . . . Who You? Part-II

It was heartening to see how sometimes our lives . . . normal lives can take so much of a beating because of love. My mind had suddenly wandered off to Tina, for the first time, ever since I came to Delhi. Somehow, Sushmita and Tina's presence in my life was kinda uncanny. They were not exactly friends and yet they were the sorts who filled me with warmth, whenever they were around. In fact, I looked up to them — these women — so confident, strong, the no-nonsense type and yet, so vulnerable.

We were so different and yet love or lack of it had brought us on the same platform. There was Tina struggling with alcoholism and trying to find her own space in Rajat's life. And Sushmita — in love with a man — who didn't want to marry her. Then there was me, who didn't even know what to do with the love that exists and the love that was so not a part of me. Is this why we women sometimes take up smoking and drinking? I wondered as I watched Sushmita's soft skin glisten in the mild sun of January. With smoke ringlets covering her face and *chai* in another hand, she enquired, 'Hey baby . . . off to an assignment?' I actually was running late but I cannot ignore her presence.

'Ah . . . yeah . . . remember I am supposed to meet that theatre guy who just launched his own Broadway musical theatre in London?'

'Oh . . . you are talking about Rajneesh Ruia, right?'

'Yup . . . so I have to meet him at his place. I better rush, John must be waiting. You know how cranky he's become lately.'

'Baby . . . these photographers have always been the crankiest lot in any newspaper. Imagine taking instructions from someone ten years your junior!'

'Hmmm . . . you are right . . . don't they just keep whining all the time?'

And we let out a giggle as I bid a hurried goodbye to meet my interviewee for the evening.

'And good luck with Rajneesh . . . he's a charmer ok . . .' Sushmita shouted out while I descended the stairs.

I chuckled.

Rajneesh Ruia's house was done up so artistically that one look at it and you knew it could only belong to someone as artistic as him. Although he was not a hot-shot in Delhi, he was well respected among the theatre and television artistes in the city. To top it all, he had a wife who any man would love to show off. We often carried their pictures together . . . sometimes six columns, sometimes full page . . . whether they deserved it or not was another issue.

And Sushmita was right. Rajneesh was quite a stunner. He had chosen an orange *kurta* for the photo shoot. So after spending about half-an-hour with John, he and his wife now turned to me. They laid out a lavish spread of Swiss chocolates, assorted biscuits and hibiscus tea to go with it. I was impressed with their hospitality, especially since many interviewees treat journalists as their private servants and even express the desire to read the raw copy before it goes on print. While some literally order us around, others have a smooth way of getting into the limelight. They befriend you first, praise you, pretend they are your greatest friends and once the 'bond' is established, they slowly and cleverly push their case 'even if it means getting a two-column story'.

Right, so I was getting somewhere with Rajneesh and his wife and I was so smitten by this artiste's charm that I secretly wished the woman away. Sushmita had rightfully cautioned me. He could have a sizzling effect on any girl even twenty years younger than him.

'So you have been covering theatre, huh?' he gently enquired.

'Actually no . . .' And before I could mutter further, the wife heaped a plate of biscuits in front of me.

'Oh . . . well . . . how kind of you . . . thank you,' I didn't know what else to say to this display of affection that I honestly didn't know how to reciprocate.

One hour up. I felt we were dragging the conversation. Basic questions asked. Personal note exchanged about him and his wife. And I decided to call it a day.

Rajneesh promised to keep in touch with me, while his wife seemed more than willing to even give me a drop till my office. I disagreed. My princely, little car was enough.

Back to the office, Sushmita was waiting for me to unload all the details about my interview. 'How was the dude? Was his wife bitchy? Did he flirt with you? Did you fall for him? Did he ask you out . . . ?' She wanted to know everything and was rather upset when I told her that it was an interview that was as plain as it could be. 'Alright baby . . . now get inside quickly . . . the ramp-scorcher is waiting for you.' I knew Ishita was waiting for me and had not asked me to split . . . so I was supposed to get back to work and file the story for the next day.

'Hey Radhika . . . how was Rajneesh?' Ishita was curious to know even before I had entered the news room.

'Oh yeah . . . just about ok . . . nothing great!' I told her honestly and then feared that she might hack my copy to unrecognisable proportions. So before I could sell my story further she ordered me to churn out a 300-word copy. 'Not a word more . . . OK!'

I secretly hoped that at least this time Ishita would like what I wrote. She didn't. Or somewhat did, but declared that I didn't have a nose for news. 'Alright, the Broadway launch . . . what else did she expect me to write other than that? His house, pets, exotic biscuits, arm-candy wife or the orange *kurta*?'

'Story Radhika . . . story . . . where's the story? Ishita thundered at me.

'The story is the Broadway. . . .'

'Oh! Now will you grow up? Who wants to read that? Who wants to even know what he's doing in London. I want to know what he does in Delhi. Who is he currently sleeping with? What colour dress did his wife wear and did you feel the cold vibes between the two of them? That's the story Radhika . . . that's the story,' Ishita was loud enough — like she always is — for the entire office to know who this Rajneesh guy was.

I was again silent but didn't quite believe that *this* is what Ishita actually wanted me to write. Not that I was upset. I was seriously puzzled about my capacity to distinguish between what's news and what's not.

Surprisingly, by the time the copy was finally edited, it was an alarming 500 words. 'Where did she get the extra 200 words from Sush?' I asked her rather bewildered.

'From her own sources baby . . . Well, didn't you know that Rajneesh and Ishita once dated and she still has a huge soft corner for him?' she asked.

'Ummm . . . well, I don't Sush and I fuckin' don't have the balls to even debate about the authenticity of my copy,' I flustered.

'It's the wisest thing to do . . . at least till you are considered old here. So keep quiet and let things go the way they are. If Ishita says jump, jump. If she says sleep, sleep. Just make sure you don't do that with Rajneesh though, or she might put you to sleep forever!' She laughed and I simply raised my eyebrow and let out a crooked smile.

Next day, the Ruias woke me up at 8 in the morning and Rajneesh thought I sounded sexy in my husky tone. 'Dinner tonight?' he asked. And before I knew, I had committed for a 7 o'clock rendezvous at Le Meridien.

I wanted to make excuses and find ways to avoid this meeting. But I couldn't. I didn't.

Journalism rule number 13: Write for your bosses first, readers come later.

14

Writing . . . Who You? Part-III

I didn't talk to Sushmita about my dinner with Rajneesh. I wasn't sure how she'd react; she might just label me as an 'easy come, easy go', but I had a nagging urge to tell her everything, especially after what transpired between me and him that night.

The dinner was a quiet one and thankfully Rajneesh was not accompanied by his shadow-cum-wife. I had decided to go Indian with an all-black ensemble, but only to match his very ethnic style. This is proof that I'd started to grow fond of him as I wanted to do things, look the way and talk the language he liked.

Our conversation mostly revolved around theatre and a wee bit about his relationship with his wife, which by now I came to know was sour. But then I wondered the obvious . . . why was she always around him when things weren't so hunky-dory? I thought it was too early to ask him that and I kept silent.

At that moment, I didn't care how they got along. I threw stolen glances at Rajneesh and was completely swept away by his deep eyes, beautiful, long fingers and the cleft on his chin. The chromosomes in me yelled to leap out and hold every part of his body. And while I was playing the 'control' freak, he turned around to say, 'You look beautiful. Can we continue meeting more often?' I blushed. I don't remember ever having blushed so much . . . not even with Sameer.

For a week, we exchanged regular texts, calls and indulged in extensive orgasmic g-chats. There were times, when I had to stop chatting with him during my working hours – to avoid distraction.

Till now, we had not touched each other. However, I wouldn't have been surprised about the wild love I'd have made with him, had he initiated even once. Two weeks into this fantasised camaraderie, and one day Rajneesh decided to come out real. 'Gorgeous, do you think you can carry the story about our next production slightly bigger than the three columns you normally give?' he asked casually.

'I don't know Neesh . . . but let me figure out what can be done,' I carefully avoided taking Ishita's name.

Exactly one week after the story was out, Neesh dahling's behaviour was not very difficult to gauge. He was frenzied about seeing his name in print, posing with his wife to add that extra glamour, and was simply using me to build a permanent rapport with *The New Press'* features section. He didn't want to do it through Ishita, so he did it through me.

I was not sad; I was angry and decided to stop doing any story that had to do with him or his theatre group, even if it meant going against Ishita's wishes. I was ready to face the flak. If blonde beneath the bleach was anything to go by . . . he was the bastard beneath the bonhomie.

Sushmita guffawed at me when I narrated the entire episode. And thank God she didn't label me. 'And, are you surprised baby?' She let out the laughter of a seasoned reporter. 'Baby, you just have to learn to decipher between friends and those who claim to be friends.' My eyebrows arched and nostrils flared. There was nothing more I could do.

Meanwhile, I was faring better with Ishita. She still continued to dislike what I wrote, but there was a pattern she followed. Sushmita was right – it was done to every newcomer. This was Ishita's way to exercise her authority.

But, whether she liked it or not, my way to get even with her was not to retaliate but to flood her with many stories. This ensured that she was compelled to carry at least five every week. And I was bang on target. On a particular day, there was a blank page and we carried four stories, and all four bore my byline. Was I proud of myself? Yes I was. From being rubbished off as someone with no nose for news to being asked to do special-page stories by Raja and Akhilesh, I think I had come a long way.

I continued doing almost *any* story – food reviews, celebrity interviews, launches – just about anything, and I was happy. Just that I was cautious never to fall prey to more Rajneeshs.

Journalism rule number 14: You just have to learn to decipher between friends and those who claim to be friends (says Sush).

15

Coming of Age

My stay in Delhi was getting increasingly comfortable. What repulsed me earlier seemed comical to me now. In fact, I had fallen in love with the city like never before. My varied interviews took me to places I rediscovered with such keen interest that I wondered if this was the same city I had hated so terribly. It was. And, now, it will continue to be the city closest to my heart.

Be it the world's best mutton stew at Kareem's, opposite Jama Masjid or a sunny evening at India Habitat Centre, the *desi-phoren* land of Paharganj or short spins around India Gate . . . I was everywhere — running, meeting deadlines, braving the traffic and most of all, enjoying this new found *joie de vivre*. I love this French phrase. No other language can describe it with such precision.

And like you can never quite get over your first love, I missed Pune too. But for now, I wanted to savour a love affair with my current paramour.

Work was great. Two years on and my itch to 'do more' led me to quarter-life crisis. During this I-have-proved-myself mode, I realised that there were other areas of my life which were screaming for attention. To begin with, my body was knocking hard against my clothes, so I needed to make a treadmill my temple; I had made no friends, so I needed to socialise more; and I was not doing anything other than work, so I needed to think about life beyond it.

Sushmita and I had started spending more and more time together. Like Jhumpa Haldar, she had neither abandoned me nor forsaken me; we both were beginning to grow fond of each other and spent many hours at the *chaiwala*. Other than the dim confines of Udupi, the *chai tapris*, right behind the dirty *galis* of ITO, were hot spots among journalists. So most of them would be found in hordes, after wrapping their first edition or waiting to release their last edition.

If our day didn't begin with a simmering cup of ginger tea, for us, it hadn't begun at all. But life said there's more to me than just this. So I jumped the bandwagon and joined *Delhi Now*.

The biggest remorse was not sitting next to Sushmita while filing stories, but that vacuum was filled during our quintessential *chai* outings. It was more needed now than ever before. To begin with, she'd hit rock bottom in her relationship and wanted to put a logical end to it. Her insecurities were growing because of its non-committal nature. During those low moments, she had often asked me, 'Baby, am I so bad that he doesn't want to marry me?' And, when this came from an extraordinarily pretty and cerebral Sushmita, I felt more than helpless. But she never let this come in the way of our professional lives and was always there to ask how I was faring at the new place.

While Sushmita was my steady support system professionally, she could naturally not fill the personal void in my life. And that void was conspicuous due to Sameer's absence.

As time passed by, our two-year-old relationship had begun to grow deeper and more meaningful. There was understanding, trust and complete companionship. While Rajat and Tina had finally decided to marry, we were yet to figure out, where we both fitted into each other's life — whether we wanted to follow the footsteps of our close friends or just remain in a loving relationship. We were unsure.

That July, just four months before I was to move back to Delhi, Sameer left for Australia.

'Sweetheart, this is gonna be a tough call for me but I have to do this for us,' he said.

'I understand but I am scared. What if you grow out of this and I don't . . . what if you stopped loving me and I pined for you . . . what if you decided to never come back . . . what if . . .' and he kissed me. Sameer's consistent nibble forced me to stop and do what was needed. Our lovemaking pattern was very unique. We often loved being child-like in bed and indulged in a fool's talk and games. However, this time it was different. We were acutely aware that this might be the last time we would ever make love. If I wouldn't miss our intense lovemaking, I was sure to miss his hugs the most. They have always given me a sense of security and great comfort, when I am happy or sad.

'This is important for us Raddy . . . we need to figure out where this is gonna go. I will be away from you for just two years and that is enough time to find out where our relationship is headed,' he cooed into my ears while still massaging my breasts.

'I know you have said that once. But aren't we gonna put our relationship at stake?' I enquired with a visibly turned-on expression.

'OK Raddy, leave journalism and come with me to Australia. Stay with me there.'

'Tch . . . you know I cannot do that. It has taken me a lot to build my career and you know how important it is for me to be in Delhi. Too much gone to reach where I am today,' I said, almost irritated.

'But am I complaining? All I say is that let's try this out. Remember sweetheart, if we ever decide to never come back to each other, we will know that we were *not* meant to be, and if we do, I promise you, you will have a lot of hard work to do in bed . . .'

We laughed out loud and made love again, but this time with a sense of delight. I felt surprisingly lighter after this conversation and was convinced that a relationship as serious as this deserved a 'let go' treatment.

I luckily had no time to ponder over Sameer's absence. One, I had professional pressures to deal with. Two, I was happy to be 'physically' single again. Too much work was a blessing and it came at a time when my mind might have driven me insane, thinking about Sameer.

But momsie often wondered why I was investing so much on a person who might or might not marry me even after two years. I wanted to tell her that I wasn't sure about it myself, but for now I had a demanding profession to keep me busy and moreover, I wasn't *over* Sameer. 'Why would I be over him when we never even had so much as an argument?' I often asked my parents.

To which they coolly said, 'Then what if he says "no" to you after he comes back?'

And I often told them what Sameer had said before he left, 'If we ever decide to never come back to each other, we will know that we were *not* meant to be together.'

The statement was like tonic to me. The wonders it did to my confidence were immeasurable. I was ready to not see Sameer even for ten years. I just trusted our love so much. I was in love and no reasoning was to ever work for me.

Journalism rule number 15: It's great to make sense . . . sometimes.

16

Don't Join Them

By now I had learnt to throw my weight around. Ravish Mathur, editor of *Delhi Now,* had called me early one Friday morning and wanted to have an urgent interview. He also wanted me to meet Veronica Kutty. And since Veronica, the managing editor was time-pressed, I was expected to reach the *Delhi Now* office in exactly an hour.

I was damn excited about meeting Veronica. Not just meeting, but I had this secret desire of working with her. She was a giant of a lady and needed no introduction. There was not a single, wannabe journalist who had not grown up reading her column *Kutty's Kut* and I had naturally fed on them too.

I revved up my car and in between managing time and thrill, I sped towards the 'no entry zone' close to Connaught Place. And what followed next were the *thullas*. But I was not going to let anyone dampen my spirit that morning, at least not when I was going to meet Ms Kutty.

The traffic cop stopped me and asked for my licence. And to my horror, he pocketed it as soon as it was trustfully placed in his hands. 'Sir . . . *galti ho gayi* . . . *licence toh de do wapis* . . .' my pleading guilty did not help . . . this was till I decided to turn the tables. 'Sir, *yeh Press ki gaadi hai* . . . I was on my way to an urgent assignment . . . now if you decide not to hand back the licence, don't blame me for what you'd see in the newspaper the next day . . .'

'*Sahi hai* . . . you people run the country in the name of Press,' he grunted and grudgingly handed back the licence. I sped off with a conceited smirk.

I was, however, part-guilty and part-angry for what had just happened. But I had to do what I did. I had 'scribe'-d off successfully and knew exactly how Sushmita would react after hearing the incident. With a cigarette in one hand and *chai* in the other, the friend would chuckle, 'Baby . . . you are learning to be a journalist now *haan* . . .'

Even before these thoughts about Sushmita or my 'courageous' act crossed my mind, I shut them out. Everyone was not like Triple S. I didn't want Ravish to wait for me and most of all, I didn't want the super scribe to leave counting her minutes waiting for me.

So, when Ravish did introduce me to Veronica, I wasn't sure if I should do a tribal dance in her admiration and tell her that she is my She Woman. I did none. I meekly sat down on the couch next to her and Ravish said, 'Meet Veronica Kutty . . . she is . . .'

That was a cue. 'Of course sir, I know her! I have grown up reading all her articles and can't help but wonder where she gets those superb ideas from. I think there is so much to learn from you ma'am, you are my icon!' Veronica grinned – the smile of a superstar thronged by her craziest fan and I was ashamedly aware of the fact that I had just mimicked Ishita during her Salman-stricken phase.

This was my second round of embarrassment since morning. But it worked, like it had previously. I was immediately offered the position of a senior copy editor, which meant, I was only next to Shri and the salary that my superstar offered me could fulfil my long awaited desire to join the hippest gym in South Delhi. 'Are you happy Radhika?' Veronica enquired, still glowing under the barrage of praises I had heaped on her.

'Of course Ma'am. . . .' I informed her, filled with gratitude.

Joining date fixed. Formalities completed. Beat assigned. Now, the only thing remained was breaking the news to Ishita, who, I was sure would be quite happy to wish me away. I was wrong. Exactly a month before I was supposed to join *Delhi Now*, I made the announcement to Ishita while driving towards the busy intersection of Pragati Maidan and simultaneously breaking most of the traffic rules by then. Jumping the red light, talking without hands-free while driving and explaining a situation to an irate boss, was definitely not the coolest thing to do, but I couldn't have figured out a better time. I thought it would be inauspicious to see Ishita's bobbing head and angry monologue before I started off with something new. The beans, however, were spilled and even seven stories, seven days a week wouldn't do the damage control.

'Ishita, I have to join them in less than a month from now,' I informed.

'You must be off your mind! Radhika, listen to me, don't be a fool. Just stay put,' she seemed impatient.

'Hmmm . . . I'd love to. You have been a great boss and I soooo loved working with you . . . but . . . can we talk once I reach office?' I almost bit my tongue at the way I eulogized about her boss-hood.

'Well, you do realise what you're getting into, right? Radhika I mean it . . . don't join them. . . .'

I was silent. The car behind me had begun honking frantically. But confidence is the key to survival in Delhi and I didn't budge from where I had parked. Instead, in typical Delhi style, I signalled him to move ahead from the other side. I had a simmering conversation to take care of.

'This will mean the end of your career in journalism and I mean it,' Ishita warned.

Perhaps her physical absence gave me the confidence to mouth my lines now, 'Ishita, my decision is firm. I have already signed my papers there.'

'Ummm . . . OK. As you wish then!' This was not what I'd expected out of a boss who didn't quite like my work and who was now hell-bent on making me feel wanted, special and whatever. And then it continued, 'You're one of the best reporters we have, Radhika, and you are so good with the pages . . . *Delhi Now* is new in the market; it will screw up your career. Tell me should I speak to Raja about your promotion? Pay hike?' I was embarrassed at Ishita's extreme anxiety. I was aware that no one in the features team really cared about her unreasonable professional demands and no one actually took it upon themselves to fulfil it, whatsoever.

The stars it seemed worked well for me that day. I didn't have to meet Ishita and when I confirmed the news to Sushmita, who naturally knew about my moves, she gave me a light squeeze. But unlike mine, she didn't carry the slightest I-will-miss-you expression. 'Oh baby . . . I am just a block away. All you ever need to do is give me a tinkle. Come to the *chaiwala* and even before you blink, I will be there.' And she was indeed always there whenever I 'needed to talk'.

Veronica Kutty's world beckoned me and there was no way I was going to stop.

Journalism rule number 16: Don't waste time beating them, just join them.

17

Firangi Date-a-Thon

My decision to remain single while waiting for someone did not necessarily mean that I was not going to date, dine and drink with other men. While my heart completely belonged to Sameer, I was also willing to make the most of the glamour and importance attached to being in journalism.

I was to meet my Croatian crush Andro Boko one evening for an interview. Like most of my other interviewees in the past, this young author from Zagreb was a strikingly charming man with a mission. He was staying at India International Centre and proposed a cup of coffee after we finished the interview. I was game because I was hungry and enjoyed dining at the garden space in IIC. After John left us, Andro and I were alone and since he was a celebrity figure in Croatia, I was naturally elated that he chose me over the other female journalists. I was cautious, post the Rajneesh episode, so displayed no signs of being either smitten or vulnerable. My funda was becoming increasingly clear — if men flirted, I flirted back. No emotional hang-ups, no love loss. However, Andro had other concerns and *I* was to be the subject of his next book. 'Yeah . . . you heard it right my Indian beauty,' Andro's voice was playful, so I didn't mind engaging in a flurry of questions that he bounced at me.

'But why me? Neither am I going to die for anyone nor compel anyone to die . . . I haven't even achieved any extraordinary feat or won too many prizes . . . then why me?' I asked Andro.

'Oh my Asian beauty . . . you have no idea about the fire you possess, I was attracted to you the moment I set my eyes on you. I really want to know how you became a journalist,' said Andro, looking straight into my eyes.

'*Matlab*? I mean . . . I became a journalist because I wanted to be one.'

'But how do Indian women become journalists? They have too many responsibilities to share, too many hardships to bear,' he almost looked sullen and frowned with concern.

'My dear Andro, it's very simple. We are modern women, independent and hard-working. Plus, times in India are very different now. Women today are far more self-sufficient.'

'Whoa! So I can see an independent, self-sufficient and modern woman talking?'

'Yes . . . why not? You could say so.'

'So, be my muse.'

I smiled, not really sure what else to do.

'You have no idea! This topic will sell like hot cakes in Croatia.'

'Topic? You mean my being a journalist is a topic?' I was still bemused by Andro's hyper enthusiasm.

'My Asian beauty, just imagine a woman journalist in India braving all odds against the male-dominated society . . .' His voice almost trailed off as if he was mouthing a monologue for an eighteenth century play.

We never spoke about 'the book' again. Andro never wanted to. And I was too embarrassed to even think about it.

Four years had passed by since. Andro has still not written the book. Maybe he's looking for more Asian muses.

Out of the ones who called me their muse, Mickey Staaik, the stern-looking Israeli was the best.

That night after I returned home, exhausted from Hanukkah's celebrations with the Jews, I was surprised when I received Mickey's call even before I entered my room. His voice was serious but warm. And he had a funny way of saying my name. It was as if invisible hands pulled his cheeks while he said my name — 'Raedeeka'! 'So I want to thank you Raedeeka for coming over tonight. Sorry, I was being too inquisitive about the story.'

'Oh . . . come on! It's alright,' I was still pissed with this guy and didn't see myself going beyond this. And it didn't. Only for that night.

Next day, I got a call from him again and again the next day and again the day after that. So practically Mickey had started calling me every day, but I was relieved that he never showed any interest in coffee, drink or other sundry activity.

I spoke to Mickey more out of professional compulsion and hated myself for this. But one day, exactly after two months of verbal torture, this unfriendly Jew asked, 'Raedeeka, do you want to visit Israel?' Of course I want to. Is that a thing to ask? 'Like, what do you mean?'

'I mean what I say Raedeeka.' Oh God! This guy loved to say my name so often and that irritated me even more.

'But what for? How? When?'

'Hang on dear . . . I know you don't like me at all, but I do like you very much and want to apologise to you by sending you to Israel.'

'What? Apologise by sending me to Israel? But "apologise" for what?'

'I think I have just been plain mean to you. I doubted your professional capabilities.'

'Huh? It's alright, chill!' I almost shouted at him.

Am I the only exception to come across such mentally-derailed, emotionally-charged humans, I wondered. But I didn't want to delay this further. So after befriending Mickey the way it pleased me, I was on my way to Israel for a two-week stay.

It was only much later that I even bothered to find out what Mickey does for a living and wanted the earth to swallow me when I came to know that this strange man was actually a hotelier, based out of Tel Aviv and had a tie-up with the embassy to send more and more Indians for religious and cultural exchange to Israel.

Under normal circumstances, Mickey should have become a friend now. But destiny decided to spare me the trouble! After a memorable stay at Mickey's 'chosen' land, he and I lost touch. He vanished from my life almost as quickly as he came into it.

The brown-black connect between Charlie Ogbeche and me was immediately established when we first met during a one-on-one interview at Hotel Ashoka. Charlie was on a week-long tour to India and Delhi was his first destination. This South African was a magician and was known for his skills in hypnotism as well.

We were scheduled to meet by the poolside and as always, I was accompanied by John. Charlie greeted me with a rose (like he must have the numerous other women journalists who came) and out of courtesy, I tucked it between my index and middle finger. Charlie was no looker. But, his face lit up when he smiled, while narrating volumes about his magic shows all over the world. He looked rather teenaged with his pimply face, straw hair and a brightly-coloured African traditional dress that loosely resembled a kurta-pyjama.

Without losing much time, we were straight at it. While the PR guys, who handled Charlie's stay in India, were too keen on the hypnosis being tried out on me, I was reluctant from the fear of babbling anything under a semi-conscious state. I relented anyway.

'Ok R-a-deeka . . . shut your eyes and visualise flying doves . . .' he tried hard to get me into a trance. 'Now, imagine the happiest time you had . . . your childhood, first kiss, mother's hug, chasing the balloons, eating lollipops. . . .' While he spoke in his thick Afrikaans accent, I fell more and more sleepy. But, I was aware of the prying eyes of the PR guys who by now were watching me diligently and even wished to take photographs, and that I strongly resented.

So I imagined everything — right from chasing bubbles, Sameer and I making love, to listening to bed-time stories from popsie, and hanging out with Rajat and Tina . . . but Charlie's tone was so animated and jocular that although I felt heavy in the head, I was constantly distracted by voices around me and I opened my eyes in the middle of the session.

'Oh what happened? Why did you do that? You were doing so well!' Charlie looked at me a tad bit disappointed.

'I am sorry Charlie but this isn't working well for me,' I meowed.

Charlie gave me another psychic glance that suggested I was a hard nut to crack. And, after we were through with the interview and enough volunteers willing to be hypnotised — whose pictures John took fervently — Charlie took my email id and promised to be in touch.

He did. Exactly two weeks after he reached his hometown in Johannesburg, he wrote a long mail that spoke about the importance of hypnotism and I sensed that Charlie was actually 'humiliated' by his inefficiency to take me to another world. He wrote to me every day and sent links related to magic and power of hypnotism. While I trashed most of these mails, there was one particular mail that didn't look like a forwarded one and that I gaped at, almost the whole day. And this was another Charlie.

His mail read:

'Hello R-a-deeka darling,

Hope ur doing good. . . .

Just a sudden urge to meet you and spend some brilliant moments with u. . . .

But I know that is not possible . . . not possible at least immediately!

Wonder if I could try hypnosis over you, over the Net? GAME? Tell me what you think . . . I obviously want to see how powerful my therapy is.

Love.'

'Fuck is!' is all that I wrote back. I never heard from the 'magician' again.

While I narrated the incident, bit by bit to Sushmita, we laughed at Charlie's sheer audacity while the 'magic' of the screwdriver had started working on us.

Journalism rule number 17: Please do not entertain weirdoes; we are weird enough!

18

Kiss My Ass

The exuberance at *Delhi Now* was so infectious that *Press* seemed like an old hag standing next to a bubbling oomph-ster. The energy was unmistakable. Other than Sonu, Salim and Rahul, I had no real hurdles to surpass. I was Veronica's favourite and Shri, if not great, wasn't mean to me either.

But there was something amiss.

One afternoon, Veronica called me to her room as soon as she had entered the office. I did the usual . . . presented the best of my smile, praised her till she grinned childishly, and only after these rituals were over, did she speak of work. She had worn black trousers with a sports tee that day and it really did look like a fashion disaster but I had gathered Veronica's weakness for excess attention and sucked up to it till she had her fill. 'I think you look gorrrrrrrrrrgeous today. And, that's such a lovely way of doing up your hair . . . just the perfect bun for the summer. And look at you Veronica, where did you buy those stilletoes? I have been dying to get them. Gosh! You should be a stylist, what are you doing in journalism?' I lied all the way . . . those loud stilettos and that archaic bun, they were totally not my taste.

'Radhika, you really think the footwear is nice? Everyone said, it's too loud but I can see that you have a true sense of fashion. And, this hairstyle really . . . it's a French bun.' Was it? She continued, 'And, since I have very long hair I just have to keep it tied up . . . Don't want to be looking so gorgeous everyday huh. . . .' and she let out a laugh that was loud enough for Ravish to walk out from his cabin to hers.

'Ok Ravi . . . I was thinking Radhika could give us a page one for tomorrow. She could do a huge piece on the thriving flesh trade at the AIIMS flyover,' Veronica suggested. Although I thought it was a nice story, it was not nice enough to be on page one. But I knew that my She Man had great sense to turn around any bit of information into a great story and knew precisely what she was talking about, at least when she talked work. I thought it was best not to interject and Ravish thought so too.

I had to start working on the story right away and the moment I saw Veronica hop over to the couch where Ravish sat, I knew it was time for me to leave her room,

Veronica had a huge crush on Ravish and made it quite evident through her body language. She often sat on the desk where he worked, held his hand on the pretext of expressing shock at a particular story and used the oldest trick adopted by most Indian women — drop her saree *pallu* and bend whenever Ravish was around. Unfortunately, it never worked for her. The smarter she was as a journalist, the dumber she was as a wooer. And Ravish, of all the men she had set her heart on, was a dedicated husband, who seemed to be completely in love with his wife — so said the picture of the two of them snuggled cozily on his desk.

While I was happy that Veronica could trust me with stories she thought were big for a tabloid, the trio was more concerned about what had transpired between me and Veronica inside her room. 'Won't you tell us?' asked Rahul sheepishly.

'Oh nothing . . . she just wants me to do a story on . . .'

Sonu smiled even before I could complete. 'Don't get into her trap . . . she'll just pile you with stories sooo much that you won't have time to edit other copies,' she cautioned.

And Salim further rattled off a tongue-in-cheek, 'Welll . . . well . . . welllll . . . We are there to clean up the shit na . . . why bother the lady for that? She's only meant for special stories you know!'

And if I had not learnt to answer back by now, I had not learnt anything in journalism. 'You are right Salim. Some people are only meant to clean up shit . . . while some people are more fortunate. My sympathies for you my dahlin . . .' And I left for a short break with Sushmita.

The *chai* break didn't turn out as expected. We walked in silence towards the *chai tapri* and Sushmita looked pale — an unusual colour for her rather glowing skin. While I had loads of unwinding to do, it seemed pointless to start any conversation that had a lot of bitching and complaining. 'What's the matter, Sush?' I enquired after ten minutes of non-verbal communication between us.

'It's getting difficult for me to forget him baby . . . I wish he realises how much I love him. Why . . . why can't he just marry me?'

I lit up the cigarette for her that day and held her arm gently.

Sushmita burst out crying. I quickly rushed her to a secluded corner, next to the huge garbage dump, away from the eyes of other journalists who might have been on with their third or fourth cuppa. 'My parents have fixed my marriage with some Bong scientist in the US I don't wanna marry him . . . I really don't wanna marry him . . . I wanna marry the man I love . . . why can't he marry me . . . tell me why . . . I love him . . .' I could have burst out crying myself. Sushmita held a special place and I couldn't see her in pain.

That day, for the first time, I was firm with my very dear friend. I didn't want to see her hurt and screw up the rest of her life for a man who had his own theories about non-commitment. 'Now you are gonna listen up very carefully, OK? I told her sternly. Sushmita took another drag with tears streaming down her pretty eyes. 'You are not gonna cry over this guy anymore . . . you have cried all these years. Has your crying changed his decision? No. So stop right here. Get a grip of your life. Check out who this new dude is and move on.'

Sushmita had stopped crying and was looking at me keenly. Maybe she was surprised at the role reversal but I didn't care . . . all I cared for was this friend who really needed to be shown the right path. 'So you're listening to me right? You are gonna break all ties with this bugger and try out the dude in the US Do it for my sake Sush . . . please . . . I can't see you cry helplessly over someone who has never given you a secure present, leave aside a secure future.'

She nodded. Lit another cigarette and threw it on an impulse. We left, without too much of a dialogue.

The clairvoyant that she is . . . even as I was climbing the stairs to enter office, Sushmita turned around and said, 'Baby . . . you're not doing anything wrong . . . if kissing someone's ass meant getting more page ones . . . so be it. You are not sleeping with Veronica, you are just praising her. So be it.' She winked and left.

I stood there a second looking at her petite frame walk by, leaving behind a whiff of cigarette smoke. One moment she wept like a child, and the other she'd taken a huge burden off my shoulders. I felt lighter in more ways than one. Something inside told me that I was going to be fine from now on, and Sushmita was going to get over her already-dead relationship.

Journalism rule number 18: Don't be guilty about kissing asses.

19

To the Past and Back

I didn't see Sushmita for over two weeks. I didn't want to mother her, so thought it was best to let her sort out her problems on her own. I knew she would.

The AIIMS flyover prostitution story had so many readers writing letters to the editor that Veronica was ecstatic. Also, this single story had doubled *Delhi Now's* readership. Shri was not sure how she should handle the sudden attention I was getting and the trio laughed behind my back and assumed that I probably slept with Ravish or Sudhakar or even Veronica to get this story. While I did none of it, I just acted smart and followed Sushmita's advice.

I laid the entire onus of the story's success on Veronica. 'You are my guru. In fact, you're the one who taught me how to write. No one could have ever thought of such a brilliant story other than you . . .' I told her till she could take it no more and actually ordered a chocolate-walnut cake to celebrate our success. While now, I was truly embarrassed, but with my She Man's hand on my head I had nothing to worry about . . . neither about the almost-charred-with-jealousy trio nor my reputation which was constantly under scrutiny.

The cake read: 'To Radhika. Give us many more page ones!!' I was honoured at this display of appreciation and somewhere scared that expectations had gone up. Sushmita's absence made things difficult for me. I had no one to share these developments with, but I knew this break was a must for her, so I didn't call her up. Instead, I called Rameshwar. This also served as an excuse to catch up with him because ever since I had moved back to Delhi, our communication had slackened, though I often thought about him. Primarily because I knew that although he had never said it, he was quite fond of me and also, because I was drawn towards the mysticism behind his nerdy mien.

My one-time lover had not changed in so many months. Not that it really mattered because that was what I had loved about him.

The phone was answered on my second try with the usual, basic pleasantries. Long silence. Long conversation. 'You will not believe this. . . .' I blurted out everything that had happened moments back in the office.

'Good good good . . . am happy for you,' he said rather plainly.

'Thanks Rameshwar . . . you know that I owe a lot to you.'

'Hmmmm. . . .'

OK. Is this all that he felt about the laurels I was bringing at my work? I questioned. 'Well . . . what else do you expect me to do? Jump, hop, jig?' Ouch.

That hurt and I decided to cut the call. 'Alright then . . . you don't seem to be in a particularly good mood. I must hang up now,' I declared.

'No wait Radhika . . . Sorry. Just that you started off on such a different note. I was actually missing you and you were on a completely different tangent.' I knew that we were in for a long conversation and I could only afford the liberty of being away from the office for an hour. However, two hours on and the conversation was leading nowhere in particular. Then Rameshwar broke the news, 'I am getting back to Suneha.'

Suneha, Rameshwar's wife had walked out on him for another man almost two years back and although Rameshwar never spoke about his married life in public, he had mentioned it briefly during one of his drunken bouts. Although Suneha's actions were nothing short of a bitch's, I had never discussed it with anyone — not even Rameshwar — because like her husband, she too was a very senior journalist and I knew it pained Rameshwar to even mention her name.

'Ok. If you think you are gonna be happy with her, go ahead.'

'I don't know if I will be happy with her again Radhika . . . but I do think she deserves another chance. Moreover, I love her.'

'Yeah I know you do.'

This was the only reason why Rameshwar had never confessed his liking towards me so strongly. The reluctance, the indifference, the sudden coldness – all this made sense to me now. Love is a funny thing indeed. It wasn't very difficult for me to let go off Rameshwar, there was nothing much to hold back anyway.

Back into the office, the fervour had still not died down. Veronica was blissfully flirting with Ravish, while Shri looked pensive. The trio had abandoned me by now.

I didn't have much to engage in either. There weren't too many events across the city during the summers, so I was racking my brains to come up with a story idea and lining up some interviews on my own. Moreover, the horrendously written copies needed some real editing; so the senseless volume of words screeched at me, while I stared at the computer screen blankly.

But I had to pretend to work in order to justify to Shri that I am not just Veronica's blue-eyed babe, but a great worker too. So I hit on the keyboard aimlessly and somewhat, hopelessly.

I remembered the first kiss that Rameshwar and I had shared and how I had actually loved and hated this guy at the same time. While I was happy that he was going to get back to a woman he always loved, I was undergoing a rush of mixed emotions. I was not exactly jealous, but just puzzled by Rameshwar's monstrous display of lust almost a year back, in the 'loveable' confines of my home . . . his eyes that spelled like and dislike towards me and his words that were nothing short of irritation. Rameshwar's irritation was amplified because he was acutely guilty of being so helplessly drawn towards me and being so helplessly in love with Suneha, both at the same time.

He suddenly popped a 'hi' to me on the gchat but I chose not to reply.

Journalism rule number 19: Moving ahead can be and should be fun.

20

Treadmill Truths

Despite Rameshwar's fleeting presence in my life, I had to constantly remind myself that I am Sameer's woman. And, Sameer is the man, my man. Although we had spoken only once ever since he left for Australia, I didn't miss his presence too much, or at least that's how I convinced my heart from falling prey to the trap of miss-and-sulk sessions. But quarter-life crisis hit back. Last time when it came, Sushmita was the leveller. This time, even she wasn't there. So I decided to change track.

I couldn't think of anything better than going ahead and fulfilling my dream of joining the hippest gym in South Delhi. And looking at Veronica, who indulged in exotic regimes of tea diet, Maggie diet and warm water diet, I was keen to shed my image from being cute to sexy.

While my world was soon finding space for sweaty boys and girls haggling over the treadmill and checking themselves out at every opportunity available, I was happy about my latest mission: be healthy, look sexy. Somehow instant rescue in the midst of an emotional turbulence always came in handy for me and most of it was surprisingly caused by a man who never exactly occupied a major position in my life — Rameshwar. And yet, he baffled me like no one else did.

Veronica, by now, had also become my unofficial dietician. So right from the time I woke up to which hard drink I drank on the previous night out, my She Man had it all charted out for me. 'Radhika, you should have mixed coconut water with vodka, will save you 500 excess calories . . . and why did you take the kebabs fried? Didn't I ask you to microwave them? Now you'll be 800 calories extra . . .' But she was clever and mean enough to not dole out the calorie secrets in public, read: Shri, who seriously needed to shed at least 50 kg! So, most of our health-cum-sex-cum-men related sessions were discussed in the closed confines of her cabin.

I had already knocked off a couple of kilos by now and graduated from a brisk walker on the treadmill to a fast runner. So I didn't care who called in at that time — if work demanded attention, it had to wait; if friends wanted to chat up, they had to wait. On a Saturday, when the gym was relatively empty, I decided to take a half-an-hour sprint. On seeing lesser number of guys who normally stole glances at girls and, guys too, I felt less conscious to run with my mouth open or smile when I knew I couldn't run further or sing when the DJ churned out a non-Punjabi track.

But after I did get down and decided to check my cell phone, there were thirty missed calls from Rajat. I darted out of the gym like lightening and hoped that everything was OK. 'Rajat, are you alright?' I asked almost breaking into tears.

'Darling . . . darling . . . darling . . . how could I be fine without my sugar honey by my side.'

'Rajat, stop kidding and come out with the truth, you asshole,' I yelled. I was not over yet. 'I had thirty missed calls from you . . . do you even realise what I thought?'

'Thought that I was dead right? How could I call you, if I were dead dumbo,' he laughed like a teenager.

'It's not funny, Rajat.'

'OK chill . . . I called you so many times because you weren't answering *na baba* . . . sorry.'

'Shut up . . . I was working out.'

'Oh whoa whoa . . . so someone's on to become sexy and all that huh?' he mocked.

'Yeah . . . why not?'

'Ok Raddy baby, give me a kissi, I have something to tell you . . .'

'Muuuuah . . . .'

'Baby . . . I and Tina have decided to marry by the month-end.'

'What? You must be kidding me, Rajat.'

'No I am not darling. . . .'

'Am soooo happy for you both, Rajat. . . .' I almost held back the tears as the gym was certainly not the place to display my emotions.

'So you've got that ass sweating out *na* Raddy . . . now sweat it more to fit into a gorgeous number for the wedding.'

'I will . . . I will . . .' I was at a loss for words. Two of the most special people in my life were going to tie the knot. I had a lump in my throat.

'Speak to Tina also darling, she might feel better.'

'I will . . . I will. . . .'

My heart ached to get out and hug Rajat and tell him that he and Tina would make the loveliest couple in the world.

I couldn't work out after that. My mind was overwhelmed and already at work to convince Shri and Veronica to let me off for twenty days. I knew it was next to impossible but I wanted to strategise, even if it meant using Veronica to my benefit.

I got back home and told momsie about it. Although she had never met Rajat and Tina, she'd heard so much about them that she could be part of my happiness. But momsie had shifted emotions as quickly as she slipped into her night gown from a heavily-starched saree. '*Beta*, when are you going to think about your own marriage? Isn't it high time you intensified your search on that marriage portal?' I hated this topic but couldn't do away with it.

'But mom, I told you *na* that I am cooperating in everything you say . . . what more should I do? Stick a placard on my chest and say marry me?'

'Your age is passing by . . . what's the point waiting for that Sameer boy? And how are you co-operating anyway? By editing your profile every day and discarding all the proposals that come your way?'

'That's not true *ma* . . . I have received thiry-three rejections so far too.'

Momsie was quiet. She had left her daughter's marriage on fate, although the thought consumed her daily. She slowly believed that I would die a cynical spinster or end up in an old age home.

Momsie wasn't to be blamed entirely, but either was it my fault. I too wanted to settle down. I missed the security of a steady relationship and missed it the most when I had to turn up alone at most of the social dos. Not that I was feeling lonesome. Sameer's presence was too strong in my life, but I did get a wee bit jealous on seeing a man chaperone his woman so lovingly.

But then, I had too much on my mind already and gymming was my latest occupation. With sweat, I let out these unsettling thoughts about my life, which were actually beyond my control. I wanted to concentrate more on what I had and do the best with it. So when I ran, I ran as if I am running towards a dream and when I stopped, I smiled and smiled as if I am the person who has just achieved that dream.

Journalism rule number 20: We all need to see a gym at least once in our lifetime.

21

I Am There . . . Almost

That day, almost after ages, I got a call from Sushmita. She was waiting for me downstairs and we instantly decided to go out *chai*-ing. So after fulfilling my commitment of giving Shri a copy on the ribbon cutters in the Capital, I couldn't wait to run down to meet Sushmita.

She was waiting for me by the stairs, with the unmistakable cigarette and pre-*chai* session's *chai*. I was seeing her almost after a month and noticed that there was something remarkably different about her. She was always beautiful, but now she looked like she's *worked* upon that beauty. There was glow on her face and a glint in her eyes. The shifty, restless demeanour had given way to a composed and graceful woman, who was just waiting to discover the world. I wanted to be a man for the moment and grab her and tell her how much of a beauty she really was, and that I would do anything to have her in my life, and that I love her . . . But I loved her anyway . . . even in the form of a woman and in all my straightness, I ran forward and gave her a tight hug.

'Oh Sush . . . how I missed you. . . .' I cried.

'I missed you too baby . . . I just wanted to figure out where I am headed and I didn't want anyone to influence my decision, so. . . .'

'Shhhh . . . it's alright. I understand.'

I had a dying urge to ask if she was out of *the* relationship, but I waited for her to download one thing at a time. 'Mark is a wonderful guy. He's half-German and half-Indian and looks after me so well,' she said. I got my answer.

The fresh splash of rain had made the otherwise messy-looking ITO service lane look messier. The tiny potholes were filled with muddy water, so one had to practically fold up the jeans or crease up the *churidaar* to save it from getting dirty. But Sushmita seemed unperturbed despite the long skirt she wore in this season. What had become of her? I wondered. The Sushmita who grumbled at the very site of a raindrop, now seemed to enjoy it as if she were always in love with the rains. Many of her other journalist friends bumped into her too and she seemed more than willing to catch up with them. The friend I knew was not like this. She frowned at the very contour of a co-journalist passing by. Well, so the journey to *chaiwala*, which normally took us ten minutes, now took us forty.

'What's all this Sush? You have changed. You are not the person I once knew.'

'You are right baby . . . The old Sushmita is dead and buried. What you see is a fresh and live version of the Sushmita I *always* wanted to be, but could never be.'

'Am so happy for you Sush. . . .'

She smiled. And, I saw that she really did care for me a lot. She bent forward and kissed my forehead. This exhibition of affection between two women might have sent other *chai*-drinking journalists into frenzy, but it was so spontaneous that it hardly mattered.

'You remember baby, how I craved for a man to love me, marry me and here I have Mark, who is just the person I always wanted. He loves me, wants to have babies with me. But the irony is that I don't really love him, I just want to be with him for the rest of my life . . . that's it.'

I knew instantly that she was not completely over her past relationship and nor the man she once loved dearly. But she had chosen to move on and used the hurt to her advantage. I was proud of her.

Shri had started editing my copy by now and frantically needed me to get back to the office. Sushmita knew that I had to leave and promised to listen to me the next time we meet.

Shri wanted to blast the shit out of me for remaining out of the office for almost an hour, but often, her words fell flat. Either she liked me too much or feared the fact that I was Veronica's guarded child. So she took out her frustration in another way. She asked me to redo the entire story. While I had written about B-grade movie stars who charged a bomb to cut a ribbon at a ceremony, she wanted me to add C-grade movie stars, and they were tough to come by. The irony was that they sought the limelight the most, and remained elusive the most.

So after an hour's scrounging around for numbers and telephonic interviews, I re-did the entire story and mailed it back to Shri. This time, however, she was happy and started explaining why she wanted me to do the story in a particular way and how Veronica gets angry when the story wasn't written in a particular manner. I knew that was not true. It was Shri's way to pit Veronica against me, but it was too late for such manipulations. And the disliking between Shri and Veronica was mutual. So the moment the latter saw me in conversation with my boss, she wanted me to come inside her cabin.

'Bitch' is all that Shri said of Veronica and let go of me.

'Come sit, Radhika.' Veronica was never this formal with me and I knew that there was something *really* official that she wanted to speak about.

'Here . . . read this.' She handed me an envelope with *Delhi Now's* monogram on it.

After I finished reading the contents of the letter, I re-read and re-read. Veronica sat across and smiled. The letter announced my promotion from a senior copy editor to an associate features editor. I got up from the couch and was blank.

'Was this for real?' I wondered. Ravish and Sudhakar had also walked into the cabin by now and congratulated me.

As an editor Ravish had to do his bit, so he said, 'Radhika, we have been very happy with your performance ever since you joined the company. You are an asset to us. This is in appreciation for the hard work you have put in.'

Sudhakar flirtatiously enquired, 'So when are you taking me out for dinner finally?'

'Ummm. . . .'

'It's OK. Now she'll take all of us out for dinner, won't you Radhika?' Veronica saved me right on time.

'Yes yes, of course. And thank you really. I don't know if I deserve this . . . but . . . .'

'Oh come on now . . . just cut the crap . . . OK,' Veronica joked.

She called out Shri's name and broke the news to her. Shri looked visibly crestfallen and congratulated me dryly.

It was a huge jump for me and it definitely meant more responsibilities and more jealousy. I was willing to take on the former and not sure if I could handle the jealousy bit, but this was what I had always dreamt of and I had finally achieved it after much trial, patience and moments of lost hope.

Life seemed slightly better and it felt like Amma's past persecution and Jhumpa's past hostility had cut a smarter and stronger person out of me. Today, I owe my success to them.

Journalism rule number 21: Keep patience, as life shows you a brighter side.

22

Do I Want This?

Perhaps, this was the only thing I had never bargained for. I had liked Shri, but now, with my new role, the rift between us was slowly turning into a chasm. And starting from the very basic, it reached levels which were very personal. Right from editing copies and assigning stories to deciding on how a page should be designed and which story should go where, Shri was beginning to have issues. So much so, trivial issues were being taken to Veronica and Ravish. They remained unfazed.

'Don't take your job too seriously, Radhika . . . Veronica is using you as her puppet,' said a seething Shri.

I just smiled, which irritated her further.

'I didn't like you assigning Rahul to cover the fashion week without consulting me,' she continued.

I got up from my seat to assert what I had to say. 'That's so totally not true Shri . . . I did ask you and you were ok about it till a week back. Moreover, during your absence I had to take a call . . . right?'

'Oh really? There's a thing called a phone, even if I am sick and on leave, right?'

'Only if you make use of it!'

'Don't you dare talk to me like that . . . I don't like being talked to in this manner,' she almost yelled at me. The entire editorial department was, by now, all ears to our verbal catfight — just short of pulling each other's hair and digging nails to draw blood out of one another's flesh.

'And . . . don't you exert your right over me like that,' I snapped.

'Well, we all know how you've come to become the associate features editor! And we know all about what you exert and on whom!'

'Let's know who and what?'

'Huh . . . I could too, if I had slept around with people.'

'Oh you shut up Shri. Mind your language. At least I am worthy enough to be slept with . . . even a dog wouldn't wanna sleep with a fat ass like you!' I think my decibel level reached such heights that even demons in hell could hear what I said. I stormed out of the news room, with legs shivering like two jelly pits. I was going to acquire the shape of a cooked noodle, from an uncooked one. I strained with the thought of being called a whore, when all I had done was a smart move of my cards. 'Was it wrong?' I wondered. 'Why would a woman co-worker, who called herself a journalist, believe that the only way to the other woman's success was actually romping with the bosses?' The entire idea was nauseating to me – not only because of the aspersions cast on my character, but also because it came from a person I genuinely liked.

Surprisingly, my She Man stayed out of it, and I was glad she did. It was that very moment I realised that Veronica was *really* smart. Our 'bonding' would have become too evident and backfired against me and her. She didn't want to lose Shri either. But Shri's growing demands, nastiness and misuse of her position had started annoying everyone. Sans jealousy, Shri was a nice human, but it was this very trait that overrode her more affable side. Well, it was for her to deal with it. For now, I was not going to function with her being around. And that put Veronica and Ravish in a tight spot. So be it!

I immediately used this as an alibi to escape to Pune. Rajat had driven me sick by his incessant calls everyday and at times I felt he wouldn't exchange the wedding vows without me. Surprisingly, it struck me that I had not enquired about Sameer's programme. I was tempted to ask but bit my tongue each time the question even crossed my mind. Ego, patience or self-restrain – I couldn't care to figure out. I was determined to attend Rajat's wedding without Sameer's presence, or rather, with Sameer's absence.

My sudden absenteeism was to have a much greater impact on the bosses than I could ever imagine. There was no reason for me to even suggest that there was a close friend's wedding and I *had* to attend it. I just shared with Veronica my discomfort . . . 'I think I need at least two weeks off.'

'I understand Radhika, but it's not gonna be very good for the team. Plus, you have many special stories lined up.'

Veronica's lollipops were not going to work for me. 'I am too perturbed by the way things have moved ever since I got a promotion. The best is, I move away from the situation and let Shri take control. She's been here longer than me and it's natural for her to feel her throne shaken.'

'Screw her Radhika . . . screw her . . . that woman I tell you. I could chuck her. . . .'

'No . . . I respect Shri, in spite of what she's done. She's excellent at her work and has never harmed me in a manner of speaking.'

'Well . . . if you insist. *Chalo*, anyway . . . take the two weeks off. It will do you some good.'

'I will not be available on the phone either.'

Veronica smiled and chuckled, 'Don't be. Who's gonna miss you here, anyway?'

We both lightened up the intense mood by sharing a giggle.

I was to leave for Pune in exactly a week from now and I found myself already running around for the designer outfits I was going to wear at the wedding. A mix of relief and excitement had started dawning upon me. I was relieved to move away from my forced 'whoredom' and excited to enter the circle of love that secured me, protected me and was unconditional. There was another gnawing fear that spread its fangs all over my body — meeting Sameer. I was uncertain about the future we once dreamt of and now, unsure what the future would be. I was going to ask this snake to shut up and crush it with all my might, but its strength overpowered mine. And I let the snake be, even if that meant choking myself once in a while.

There was no doubt, I was always confident about Sameer and my relationship with him, but it would be another thing to see this man in flesh and blood after three years . . . this man with whom I had spent sleepless nights, making wild and tender love. Still, I was adamant to not ask him about homecoming.

My heart leaped with unleashed joy as I watched a tiny Pune from the aircraft. Soon I would dissolve in its dust, moody rains and the many smiling, yet indifferent Punekaru.

If I had not formed this rule by now, there was no way I was going to survive further.

Journalism rule number 22: Learn to say 'get lost' when you really want someone to get lost. 'Fuck-off' sounds even better.

23

There's No Tomorrow

I was tad disappointed to not find Rajat at the airport, to receive me. I had to seldom ask him for anything. He was the kind of guy who always did things without being told. But I quickly gathered my sulking thoughts and deduced that he was going to get married and it was wrong to expect anything from him, especially when the wedding was just a week away.

However, in the middle of my bargaining session with the auto *rickshawwallas*, I spotted a tiny figure run towards me. Tina? 'Wow . . . is that you girl?' I was left gaping as I saw this crazy-for-short-things, alcoholic of a girl turn into someone I couldn't even recognise. The girl was wearing a well-sequined *salwar kameez*, two gold bangles and had streaked hair, in place of a panty-peeping skirt, African beads and loosely-tied bun. No doubt Tina looked even more beautiful than what she originally was.

'God! Tina . . . look at you!' I gushed.

'Stop embarrassing me, Rads. Anyway, hop over. Hope I am not late. Your friend will kill me if he finds out that I made you wait.'

'*Arre* . . . but I was expecting neither of you to come. You guys are getting married and it's not good for you two to move out much now.'

'Cut the crap Rads . . . Coming to receive you was a good chance to get out. I was getting bored as hell. Rajat has abandoned me altogether now.'

'That's because you're going to be his forever, sweetheart.'

'Hmmmnnn . . . I couldn't be happier. He's wonderful indeed.'

I agreed no less. Such is Rajat.

As Tina drove me towards the house, many thoughts made way through my mind. On an impulse, I spoke my heart out to Tina. 'Is this what love does to you?' She looked baffled. Tina was not the intense-kinds who would spend hours brooding over something. She was not shallow either. She just didn't take life too seriously. 'Ah . . . I mean you've changed completely. You were so different and look at you now.' My mind raced back to Sushmita who had undergone a similar metamorphosis. And I really wondered if commitment-laden-love changes your bearing, right from the way you dress up and eat to the way you talk to others . . . is this love?

I knew I could never get a suitable answer from Tina, so I was going to wait for Sushmita's explanation till I reached Delhi.

The pre-monsoon showers had wiped Pune clean. While Punekars hated the city during this season, I loved it. And this time too, I was not going to leave a single chance to slip into tattered jeans and *chappals* and soak my skin wet in the rains.

With the exception of a few new malls, Pune had not changed much. Its people were the same, its unruly traffic, pot-holed roads and the many memories that sent me back in time, were all the same. I had the same feeling . . . just the kind I had when leaving the city for Delhi. Pune was like an old paramour, always there when you wanted to be covered with the warmth of a bosom. But would we ever be the same again? Rajat and Tina getting together, Sameer was gone and I was determined never to leave Delhi again. And for whom? There was no sense of loss, just an acute sense of a belonging, for the one that I longed for.

My heart couldn't gather the words to reach my throat and at least enquire if Sameer was coming or not. 'And what was with these people anyway . . . why wasn't anyone talking about him either? No one had even mentioned Sameer . . . not even once. Were Rajat and Tina so lost in their wedding preparations that they had forgotten a close friend?' None of these thoughts were naturally going to reach anyone. Moreover, Rajat-Tina were not the kinds to forget loved ones.

I thanked Tina as I entered the house. I was going to make the most of my time alone here.

The next few days were going to be busy, so I needed to catch up on as much sleep as I could for today. Coffees, luncheons, lounges were out . . . I'd have to meet Rajat in a family setting now.

It was difficult to tell when I fell asleep while watching the rain drops from my bedroom's window. I slept the whole night, only to get up at 5 am and see some thirty missed calls from Veronica, Rajat, banks and mobile companies.

By noon, I was ready to rule the world again. Veronica needed fresh inputs on the BPO scam story, which I gave her over the phone. Rajat was mad at me for not staying at his place — I didn't give in. And the rest, I didn't care.

I slipped into a tie-and-dye saree with heavy *kundan*-work jewellery and decided to brave the rains. Kanta *bai* came in handy to get the auto at my doorstep. I love her. 'Baby . . . *neet zha* . . . too much rain. Don't spoil your saree and make-up,' she ordered.

'Don't worry Kanta *bai* . . . I am not a kid anymore *na*. . . .'

I couldn't wait to leap into Rajat's arms.

Journalism rule number 23: No rule! Let the mind be clustered at times.

24

And I Danced All Night

It took me exactly thirty seconds to take a straight dive into Rajat's outstretched arms. While his many relatives might have found this totally scandalous, Rajat and my relationship went beyond sexes. We hugged each other hard, danced around in circles and I sat myself down on the coolest place in this world — Rajat's lap. By now, the relatives were gaping and I might have surely been termed as a man-snatcher, but we both couldn't care less.

'Raddy baby . . . you have to perform an item number on *Hips Don't Lie*,' he declared suddenly.

'Yeah sure . . . dance . . my foot.'

'Yes . . . that's what I want — your foot to dance. Now come on darlin', aren't you gonna do this much for me?'

'Rajat, that's an unreasonable demand. You want me to be the laughing stock in front of all your relatives?'

'Oh screw them honey . . . tomorrow is the cocktail night.'

'What? Did I just hear tomorrow?'

'Ye . . . ah . . . to . . . mo . . . rrow.'

'Screw you. Nothing doing.'

'Please baby . . . how else are you gonna make me happy?'

'Ah! Jeez . . . call some dancers.'

'Raddy . . .' Rajat can be so authoritative at times that convincing him could be next to impossible. And there was no way I could change his mind about the strange fixation of seeing me dance on *Hips Don't Lie*.

'Hmmmnnn . . . am doing this only for you. OK.'

'Yippeee . . . I so love you my baby. . . .'

'Go to hell.'

'Muuuah.'

'Ok, meet Sandy. He's gonna teach you some dance steps. You guys get the hell outta here right now and get your act together for tomorrow night.'

I scrunched.

Sandy was an attractive-looking choreographer who had a body as chiseled as a Greek God. I immediately said a silent prayer, thanking God for the kilos I had lost recently. My body was curvier, lighter and sexier and I wouldn't have to be ashamed about being lifted up or being touched at the waist.

After grumbling a bye to Rajat and his parents, I headed home with Sandy on his Enfield. It was my first time on this bike and I loved the drizzle that played hide-and-seek as we rode at full speed. I nudged Sandy to ride faster from the fear of spoiling my saree.

'Alright . . . so this one . . . this two. Left ahead. Now swirl right.'

I wasn't so bad at following the dance moves, but Sandy was way too fast and I had a lot of catching up to do.

'Here you go . . . a one, two, turn . . . and a three, four bend.'

He clapped at every move that I got right.

While all my senses concentrated on looking sexy as I followed the steps obediently, a part of me was also warm. This was the first time I'd ever come this close to a man after Sameer and there was definitely a lot stored up within. There was a time when Sandy and I were so close to each other that I could feel the thing between his legs. No. It wasn't hard. This was Sandy's job. He might have trained a dozen girls before me. But for me, it was pure carnal pleasure. It was this time that I realised how trapped water inside a faucet must feel — waiting to gush out, waiting to fill up an entire basin.

My breasts were stiff and I wanted to grab Sandy by his neck and smooch him hard. I didn't. There was no way I was even going to hint that we could go to bed and forget that anything ever happened between us. I disguised myself to be a naïve pupil. We danced the whole night and were ready to pull off an excellent show for the night that followed.

The *Hips Don't Lie* jig went off so well that we got an encore and meanwhile, Sandy was turning out to be a great companion too. He filled the vacuum that Rajat-Tina-Sameer's absence had caused. And Sandy was not an off-the-shelf choreographer. He had completed his Masters in social work from London School of Economics and was currently pursuing dance — his passion — during his stay in Pune.

The next day and the day after were fairly easy for us, so Sandy, real name: Sandeep, offered to take me out for a long ride on his Enfield. I couldn't say no to the proposition. Didn't want to.

For the next two days, we hogged on *paav bhaaji*, visited café Maha Naaz, strolled on M G Road, dined at Koregaon Park, watched Vijay Tendulkar's English adaptation of *Gidhade*, visited Shaniwar Wada and drank and danced the night away on my all time favourite TDS.

This was Pune rewound and revisited. There are many places and things you often overlook about a city when you start living in it. This time I went back to my city with the detachment of a tourist, whose remains were lost somewhere in its black soil.

The day before the wedding was so hectic that I had serious concerns about my attendance during the main do. Since I was representing both the bride's and the groom's side, I was practically shuttling from one part of the city to another. While Tina and her mother lived in Camp area, Rajat's house was located in Kalyani Nagar. The entire day, I could swear by Sandy. He not only ensured that I was picked and dropped back well in time for the *mehendi*, ladies' *sangeet* and be by Rajat's side for moral support, but also saw that I was comfortable. Since Sandy was a bike person, he seldom drove, but for my sake, managed to pull out his vintage model of Mercedes.

He and I were inseparable and yet we knew nothing about each other, other than the fact that he loves dancing and that I am a journalist. I believe in instant chemistries and that's when it really doesn't matter who the person is or where he really comes from . . . all that matters is a feeling that you like being with the person . . . you want to go on being with that person.

Although Rajat and Sandy barely knew each other, my trust in the latter gave Rajat the confidence that I was in safe hands. 'I feel guilty about not being able to spend as much time with you as I would like to,' said Rajat.

'It's ok. Don't be silly!'

'Yeah . . . but I do hope this Sandy guy is taking good care of you. Hope you guys are not being naughty,' he winked.

'Shut up, Rajat! He's a fine person.'

'Hmmnn . . . I can see you both are bonding pretty well!'

'Yeah we are . . . but. . . .' And I stopped short of words. Till this moment I'd not realised that I had developed high levels of self-restrain, coupled with an unbeatable ego. There was no way I was going to enquire about Sameer. And why should I? Had he even bothered to tell me about **his** plan?' I left in a hurry to be with Sandy again.

I was so exhausted with all the running around that all I needed was a mattress to rest my tired body on. Part of my exhaustion was also because of the heavy saree I had worn the entire day and now, I could do anything to get out of it. So, the moment Sandy and I reached home, I dashed into my bedroom, took a shower and stretched myself on the couch next to Sandy.

The obvious didn't happen. To say that I didn't look tempting in wet hair, loose-fitted shorts and smoothly moisturised skin, was incorrect, but to say that Sandy was anything but horny, was totally correct. Surprisingly, his lack of 'interest' relieved me. We took two straight shots of vodka, ate a delicious Chinese meal from Ching Land, and I crashed on the bed, only to be woken up next morning by Kanta *bai's* incessant ringing of the door bell and chants of 'Baby . . . baby. . . .'

Journalism rule number 24: Tch . . . It's wedding time! Aren't you supposed to enjoy that? Shut the rule book for a while.

25

The Ring is Mine

Sameer and I got married in the cold of December. It was the worst month to tie the knot, but between my bouts of sulks and hurried shopping, we chose December nonetheless.

I had always harboured a strong dislike for Delhi winters. They are harsh and unforgiving and if winter blues are anything to go by, I get them even before the cold waves hit the otherwise dry city. Sameer and my wedding was everything that I had *never* wanted/visualised/dreamt of. After signing on the dotted line at the court room with only four witnesses by our side — his parents and mine — we were going to fly to Australia soon after. The better part about the entire nuptial agreement was its reception.

Veronica's contacts ensured that we got married at one of the elitist places in Delhi — the Delhi Gymkhana Club — where she took over as my surrogate mother. She handled the catering, lights arrangement, music, guests, and nagged the workers endlessly over their inefficiency to get the right things at the right time. My She Man is a perfectionist and can make life hell for anyone who does not comply with her orders.

Momsie and popsie might have felt slightly cornered by Veronica's overpowering mannerisms and the fact that in spite of being my boss, she was more like a mother or a sister. I felt that it was actually a blessing in disguise because they would have been crushed with the anxiety of a rushed wedding and that too of the daughter who they still thought was not more than a 10-year-old. I assured them, 'Veronica was only being nice to us, momsie. Moreover, you have given me so much that it's only unfair to trouble you because Samuur is suddenly saddled on a horse!'

'I understand darling. Anyway, forget that your dad and I will sit and work that out with Veronica,' momsie said, trying to hide something.

'What happened momsie? Are you alright?'

Popsie joined in and looked rather coulourless despite the radiant, golden *kurta* he had worn for the reception. I knew what momsie was hiding, just as she knew, what I was hiding.

We three were alone in the greenroom of the club, but it seemed like I was thronged by a zillion recollections of my childhood with these two individuals, whom I would henceforth be meeting so rarely — first, once a year, then once in three years . . . then only on occasions that demanded my presence. I couldn't bear the thought of leaving them behind and started weeping almost inconsolably.

As an adolescent, I had always wanted to maintain a diary to pen down my anger, irritation, love and even hatred for my parents. I had secretly even wished that they would someday read it without my knowledge and figure out exactly what and how I feel for them. But I could never quite maintain an account of the day's feelings, events, highs and lows and whatever. I felt that was another person I wanted to write about and now another person stood tall in front of me, to remind me that I am a fake, at times a pathological liar and at other times, a bad human too . . . Right now, I had just one idea in my mind — to call off the celebrations and tell Sameer that I *have* to stay back in India, in Delhi or in Pune, wherever. I just so wanted to be close to momsie and popsie.

My going away also meant that I was going to say goodbye to journalism. I suddenly loved everything that was attached to this industry — the adrenalin rush after your name gets known by a breaking story and you have channels and other newspapers following it up and at times even calling you up to know about the sources. Or the times when your colleagues and bosses feel threatened by your presence or the way people took up journalism after you'd told them that you're a journalist. I will have to do away with everything to be with the man I love. 'So much for love!' I wondered.

Just then Veronica barged inside the greenroom and scolded me lovingly for not being ready on time. 'Out you two . . . let the girl get ready,' she commanded my parents who looked rather shocked by her free-speech. 'Ah . . . no . . . don't look so annoyed. People take a long time to get used to the way I talk,' and she started laughing hysterically.

Rajat trooped in behind Veronica and proposed to accompany me as I walked amidst the guests — a job that my She Man so wanted to do. Rajat being Rajat had the final word.

The Gymkhana lawns looked splendid at night. The neatly manicured lawns were decked up with fairy lights, the *shamiana* was erected in white satin, with a bunch of flaming lavender orchids pasted delicately on the cloth. Then there was an open bar and a live music console (the DJ played the bridal march as I walked in and quickly switched over to Hindi retro remix as soon as I settled down. Ouch!) Among a sea of faces, I could spot some known and some unknown ones. And then there was the man — my man — Sameer looking so blissfully content that I had no doubt in believing that I was what he always wanted, the first time he ever set his eyes on me at TDS. He looked at me with the same love, I had felt for him — warm, understanding, wanting, fulfilling . . . he slipped on a solitaire on my ring finger, where the wedding band already rested. 'You are mine Radhika . . . will you be mine forever?' He asked, somewhat lending the environment a *filmy* air.

'What's all this?' I asked Sameer as I looked at the crowd who stood in rapt attention and, some even smiling at the exchange of dialogues between the newly-weds.

'Let me explain this to you. . . .' Veronica was suddenly speaking on a mike, while Rajat held another one.

'We decided to have this little fun . . . so tore Sameer's pocket apart to buy his beautiful bride a raindrop solitaire ring . . .' Veronica continued with the air of a seasoned emcee.

'Now after Rads slips in the ring on Sameer's finger, we'd love to see the couple dance,' announced Rajat.

My jaw almost dropped as I looked at Tina quizzically and shot an angry yet embarrassed glance at Rajat. A) I had no ring to give to Sameer. B) I was not prepared for any sort of dance number. C) I thought this was my wedding reception and not some promotional event where I needed some emcees to amuse the crowd.

It took me a while to figure out that the rings were basically our wedding gifts from Rajat and Tina.

Our special ball dance on *Lady in Red* by Chris De Burg was just an excuse to get the crowd grooving and my friends' aim to make the reception as informal as possible was achieved.

The reception night swayed away gently, waiting for me to start my life as Mrs Radhika Khanna . . . or like Veronica insisted, 'Stick to Radhika Kanetkar Khanna.' I always smiled at the proposition of a sentence-long name.

Journalism rule number 25: Don't get too attached to your job, life has many changes to throw in.

26

~~~~~~

Suddenly So Sudden

Our prayers were answered. It didn't rain on the wedding day. There were enough showers of blessing throughout the week, so we didn't need any on the D-Day. Many guests had come from Rajat's hometown Delhi, and since weddings were the best time for Delhiites to dress up and show off, the weather didn't play spoilsport.

Tina, the bride, looked resplendent in her red-pink *lehenga-choli*, while Rajat's ensemble of a *sherwani-lungi* made him look nothing short of a nawab. I stuck to my choice of a golden saree with heavy *gota-patti* border, matched with a to-die-for emerald green *choli*. Now all we had to do was wait for the *pheras* and other ceremonies to be performed. I realised that neither Tina nor Rajat needed me around (they had a barrage of willing cousins who wanted to run errands). So I was back to being with my companion Sandy, who also looked deliciously attractive in his smart grey trousers and jacket with a shiny blue-lavender tie.

In the midst of all this looking great, helping friends, feeling nice, feeling turned-on-emotion, I had, almost, forgotten about Sameer and my eyes were fixated at the image in front of me. The contour looked like Sameer's when I saw a man hug Rajat tightly, then lift him up, then indulge in a friendly banter. I stood gaping as I realised it was Sameer, my man . . . who looked leaner, manlier and somewhat artificial. Or was I analysing him too much, even before he'd settled in? My mind was clearly undergoing a kickboxing match.

But I was right. Sameer had seen me by now. He came close to me. Shook my hand and said, 'You look beautiful.' Alright . . . so? My heart skipped a beat. 'Had Sameer really changed?' I wondered. 'And wasn't he the one who always said, 'If we come back . . . it was meant to be . . . if we don't . . .' But I wasn't getting clear signals so I decided to play along.

We hadn't spent much time together during the wedding. My doubts were being confirmed in the middle of many beliefs and an undying faith, but then I wasn't even prepared for the suddenly sudden turn of events.

I was home and looking at the children splashing water by the swimming pool. The rain had decided to become a brat once again, so it drizzled lightly and I let the soft water droplets fall on my head. I opened my arms wide and tilted my face upwards so I could feel the fresh drops of water splash on my skin as they dived straight into my eyes, nose, mouth and ears. I told myself that I was gonna be alright even if Sameer no longer felt the same way for me. I reconciled by telling myself a dozen times that I could change my mind too . . . why blame it on Sameer then?

When the doorbell rang, I knew it couldn't be Kanta *bai*. She seldom came to work in the afternoons. It was Sameer.

'Hi.'

'Hi.'

'Do come in.'

'Don't you think you've become too formal?' he asked.

I smiled because I thought he had.

Surprisingly he came out to sit with me in the balcony and asked for a cup of coffee as soon as he settled himself on the rocking chair.

Coffee done. Reminiscing about the past, done. Australia done. India done. Rajat-Tina done. Wedding done. I was getting irritated. 'Were we running out of conversation?' I wondered to myself.

Just then Sameer pulled me towards himself with a jerk, cupped my cheeks in his palms and sent me shitting bricks. 'Is December a good time?' he enquired.

To lay eggs? 'Right . . . for what?' I was still agitated.

'For us to marry.'

I was numb.

'I love you Radhika. Grow old with me. Have my babies. Fight with me. Love me. Be with me,' Sameer's eyes were moist.

I was numb.

'I have punished you and myself enough. Just say yes . . . just say yes, Radhika.'

'I love you too, Sameer. Whatever made you think I will say no? December it is. And since when did you become so poetic?'

Sameer lifted me up in his arms. We didn't make love. We were back to business with our wedding plans.

Journalism rule number 26: Didn't I say, believing is having?

27

Stilettos in the Newsroom

Back in Delhi, I had a lot of catching up to do - professionally. Veronica was waiting to pounce on me with shit-load of work and Shri looked anything but helpful. But I couldn't care less. There was a spring in my step and a lilt in my voice. I knew that my world was going to change forever and I was happy about it.

So far, no one except momsie-popsie and Rajat-Tina, knew about the latest development in my love life and although they all were ecstatic about it, they had warned me against telling anyone before it was 'official'. So I didn't and other than Veronica trying to dig the truth out every now and then, there were no apparent signs of anyone knowing anything about anyone.

Rahul, Sonu and Salim were suddenly friends now, although I could never call them one because I was aware that behind my back, they bitched endlessly about me and poured venom on me with Shri. I felt sorry to see that she was left alone since groupism was becoming evident. Life's logics can be so simple at times — people who love you for your position can never be your friends and your friends will never love you for your position. But I was here to perform my duty, so if I was made the associate features editor, I was going to treat myself that way and ensure that others treated me that way too.

I held regular edit meets (with or without Shri), demanded at least five stories in a week, suggested that their own promotions were going to depend a lot on the way they edited stories, gave headlines, wrote their copy and designed pages. The team sulked, but it didn't matter.

It felt like ages since I had caught up with Sushmita, so after assigning work to every member of the team, I quietly sneaked out to meet her. I knew I wouldn't be able to spend much time with her now, like on previous occasions, but I wanted to make the most of whatever we had. While Sushmita and I stood close to the *chaiwala* doling out details about Sameer and Mark, Shri walked in and expressed her desire to 'talk to me privately'. No . . . this was my and Sushmita's time, so I was rude enough to tell her that I would see her in the office. 'Alright, I will wait for you,' she said and vanished as suddenly as she had appeared.

Back in the office, half-heartedly, Shri pulled me aside to the cafeteria immediately. 'Listen Radhika . . . I am sorry,' she sobbed.

'Hmmnn . . .'

'I like you a lot, but I tend to get a little short of fuse,' she said half-smiling, half-sobbing.

'Alright. Forget it. But remember Shri, it's not me who makes the team, it's us. You are perhaps far more important and I really want you to realise that.'

Shri looked at me and gave me a hug.

I was relieved to have her back because this meant there was division of labour. My loving gesture towards her was not because I wanted a friend in her, but because I didn't want to lose a good worker/boss.

With Shri back in action, the work was in full swing. Features section of *Delhi Now* was taking the lead in breaking news in almost every field right from arts and fashion to books, music, society . . . we had it all. Veronica, Ravish and Sudhakar were so happy with our success that a pat on the back was becoming a common gesture for us. I was happy, also because the other side of me was also beginning to fall in place.

I resigned in the month of November. The entire December was busy and by March I joined Sameer in Australia. I drew solace from the fact that we were going to come back to India within six months and the best part was that his company had deputed him to handle operations for a month from Delhi. I couldn't ask for more.

Getting spoilt by momsie and popsie was unlimited; in between, I also made a quick trip to Pune to meet Rajat and a pregnant Tina, and Sandy, whom I had not met since I left Pune after the wedding. One month was flying by, when I most wanted it to stretch itself by a few more days.

This time, I didn't want to sulk, sob and waste time brooding over anything – I had enough time to do that in Australia. So I made sure that out of Sameer's busy schedule, he still made time to take me out for a short spin, every alternate day. He understood my requirement to still feel attached to what I was going to leave behind forever.

On one of these drives, I had a nagging urge to ask Sameer to drive a little further towards ITO. He did. 'Hey Sameer, look, that's my office! Doesn't the *Delhi Now* board look really cool?' Next to it was *The Press'* board that looked equally overpowering. Sameer peeped out, genuinely trying to seem interested. 'And look there . . . that's were Sushmita and I stood for hours . . . sharing *chai*, gossip and great friendship . . . And that's where we went to have our regular meal . . . that's Udupi and that . . . faaaarrrrrrr away is our *chaiwala* . . .' I had promised myself to allow no entry to tears in my eyes. Well, I lived up to it. I didn't cry but felt a deep sense of attachment towards this profession that not only taught me how to be a journalist but also a complete individual.

My sense of deja vu was so acute that I had to ask Sameer to take the inside lane. Right outside the office, I really hoped to bump into someone I knew, or someone I had worked with. There was no one. New faces showed up and a lot had changed in a little time. I wanted to meet deadlines again, grill interviewees with questions, get high on a byline again, edit bad stories again, walk with stilettos in the newsroom again and draw attention from everyone and more than anything else . . . just be here a tad bit more . . . again.

Sameer waited patiently for me to signal him to drive off. I looked at him and felt so hugely disconnected, just for that moment. There was no way he was ever going to understand what it meant for me, to just stand there and gloat about the fact that only the fittest survive here. A co-journalist would.

Like popsie would often say, 'How can someone as sensitive as you even survive here? Are those stories really written by you? You don't even know the roads in Delhi so well . . .' Well, I have survived and many others after me will

Sameer and I drive ahead.

Journalism rule number 27: We journalists make it a point to know very little about an extremely wide variety of topics; this is how we stay objective.*

Stay objective, anyway.

---

*The last rule has been taken from one of Daves Barry's quotes. He was an American writer and humourist.